THE TROUBLE *With* THE TRUTH

THE TROUBLE *With* THE TRUTH

EDNA ROBINSON

INFINITE WORDS
NEW YORK LONDON TORONTO SYDNEY

INFINITE WORDS
P.O. Box 6505
Largo, MD 20792
www.simonandschuster.com

ISBN 978-1-59309-640-3
ISBN 978-1-4767-9349-8 (ebook)
LCCN 2014942323

First Infinite Words trade paperback edition February 2015

Cover design: Kristine-Mills Noble
Cover illustration: © Masson/Shutterstock.com
Book design: Red Herring Design, Inc.

10 9 8 7 6 5 4 3 2 1

Manufactured in the United States of America

No matter what the clocks and calendars say...
The years between forty and fifty seem to take one.
From thirty to forty takes two; twenty to thirty, three.
From nine to nineteen takes twenty.

EDITOR'S NOTE

The visions of my mother perched on a black iron chair with a quilted back, in the upstairs "study" of our custom-designed Ed Barnes house, are burned into my childhood memory. The flat-roofed, square-box, unheatable construction, with huge picture windows, no curtains, and a kitchen the size of a closet bore no resemblance to the traditional homes on our dead-end street.

It was my mother's dream house, commissioned after she discovered photographs of Edward Larrabee Barnes's designs in the Museum of Modern Art. Feeling as if she'd found her soul mate, she called him up. Charmed by her guileless admiration, this world-famous architect not only agreed to design our house, but he and my mother collaborated to such an extent that, in my mother's telling of it decades later, they fell in love. But she was married, as was he, and it was probably a fantasy of perfect love anyway. So, she remained a "good girl."

I can see her now, seemingly in a trance in front of her big, wooden desk, an oversized green and black stoneware cup of black coffee going cold on the side of it, as she alternately pauses and erupts in furious typing. It was the late fifties, and now that I am old enough to be her mother at the time, now that I too am a writer, as well as a book editor, I look back on her strangeness, passion, absence, and burning—albeit frustrated—ambition with painful understanding.

Circa 1957 she wrote a short story, "The Trouble with the Truth," that became the first chapter of this novel. When it was published in the 1959 edition of the *New World Writing* book series, selected as one of the "most exciting and original" stories of its time by editors who had previously introduced the work of Eugene Ionesco, Samuel Beckett, Jack Kerouac, and John Wain, it seemed as if her fantasy of becoming a successful novelist was at hand. Here is her bio from that publication:

> Born in Tulsa, Oklahoma, Edna Robinson was graduated from Northwestern University in 1943. For a few years, after college, she wrote advertising copy, as well as a variety of radio and television shows; she has only recently turned to fiction. She lives in Briarcliff Manor, New York, with her husband and three small children. This is her second published short story.

She soon found an agent, completed the novel that you are about to read, and in a writer's worst nightmare of bad timing, it was optioned by Harper & Row just before *To Kill a Mockingbird* blew the literary world apart—whereupon her editor dropped the option because there just wasn't room for another period book about a single father with two peculiar children.

Life changed, another baby was born, a marriage exploded, and making a living became my mother's priority. By the seventies, she was sober and stable. By the early eighties, I was living the life I suspect she'd secretly longed for (but would not have liked if she'd had it)—writing without the constraint of dependents—and when I found an agent for my own first novel, I insisted she submit her book to him. She handwrote revisions on the yellowing, heavy bond paper with elite type from her manual Olivetti, retyped on her pica-fonted Selectric, photocopied, and when my agent rejected the manuscript, once again returned it to its crushed brown box. In 1987, my mother and I became partners to write movies after we received a Writers Guild East Foundation Fellowship that I insisted we apply for as a team. Here is the bio she wrote to try to sell our scripts:

> Edna Robinson lived all over the U.S. and attended twenty-seven schools. Early on, she wrote for radio soaps and small-town newspapers' "Society News." Later, in addition to co-heading a company that imported Argentinian Miniature Horses, she wrote comedy material for television, several of the best-known advertising lines ["Navigators of the world since it was flat"; "A kid'll eat the middle of an Oreo first..."; "Nutter Butter Peanut Butter Cookies"] while on the staff at large and small ad agencies, feature articles for horse magazines and *Sports Illustrated*, children's books for Hallmark, and short stories for adults.

Life changed, jobs changed, sickness came, and on March 26, 1990, my mother succumbed to leukemia and emphysema. She never got to publish this novel, or the one she was working on when she died. She left all her manuscripts to me, and, sadly, the second novel was mostly in her head. But this one survives.

Things are very different from the days when Edna Robinson sat on her black iron chair at her big wooden desk in an unheatable house near the banks of the Hudson River. I now make my living as an editor and, embracing the ways of twenty-first-century book production, I've decided to present my mother's 1957 novel—retyped and edited—to an unknown world of digital readers.

"A fantasy," she called it. "Oh, Betsy, it's so dated," she'd say when I asked her about it in the late eighties. "It was what I imagined a good father to be."

Fantasy, yes. My mother never experienced the kind of love you are about to read. But what a grand story.

We hope you enjoy it.

—Betsy Robinson

CHAPTER ONE: THE TROUBLE WITH THE TRUTH

My father's reason for keeping my brother, Ben, and me with him—that we were his children—was incomprehensible to our only other living relative, Aunt Catherine Tippet. In the marrow of her well-fleshed and corseted bones, she was convinced that the arrangement was inflicting irremediable harm on us, and that it was another positive indication that Walter Briard, my father, was crazy. Had she been honestly willing to take us into her own home in Sapulpa, Oklahoma, and had not Walter Briard's eccentricities been of a variety she feared would reflect unflatteringly on the memory of her poor dead sister Jen, our mother, she would have tried to have him declared unfit.

As it was, she contented herself with the performance of lesser Christian duties. Once each month she wrote a long advisory letter to all of us (on the same day she went over the accounts of her husband Joe's drugstore; "he just never had the luck the others did, in oil"), and once each year she came by bus or train—God didn't mean for her to fly—to visit us for four or five days. Since Aunt Catherine was a woman whose remarkable natural alertness was usually devoted to such tasks as making worn-out bath towels into usable washcloths, she must have welcomed these inspection trips with their implicit opportunities for travel. From the time of my birth in 1921 through my first nine years, we lived in twenty different places.

Aunt Catherine reconnoitered, and worried, in at least ten of them.

She'd arrive early in the morning with a cheap black pocketbook full of laxatives and a nervous eye for a messy desk (my father's) or hair that needed washing (mine). Ben, whom she often called "my little businessman" in a complimentary, encouraging way, would vanish and hardly reappear for the remainder of her stay except to eat and sleep. My father, after greeting her with his wrinkliest, most insincere smile, would hear from some long-lost customer he hadn't seen since his expatriate days who suddenly turned up a half-day's drive away and insisted on seeing him daily. Fred, our Welsh houseman, would have to drive him. Fred's bald head and beaked nose with the silver-rimmed glasses perched on it, and his immaculate dress made him appear rather chilly-formal. But in truth, he was warmly sentimental, almost childishly so. He loved to drive my father, had been doing it for thirty years or more, through the decades of my father's bachelorhood, and he would sprint to get the chauffeur's cap he had long ago purchased himself. So I was the one who spent the most time with Aunt Catherine.

Invariably she began our conversations by sympathizing with me. "Lucresse dear, you have *such* a cross to bear." She meant, I knew, because her sister Jen had died giving birth to me. Nonetheless, I'd let her go on, hoping she'd tell me more about my mother than that. My hopes were never fulfilled. Aunt Catherine always spoke of a young girl Jen and a young woman Jen. I knew my mother would be about as old as my father—they had married when he was fifty-two and she forty-six—and I wanted help in visualizing her, with him, when I was a possibility. Eventually, I learned that Aunt Catherine hadn't seen her sister after Jen left Sapulpa, at twenty-one, to study art in New York and subsequently in Paris, where she "met up with" my father.

Our conversations usually ended when, out of an urge to communicate on a more realistic level, I'd let slip, "When we lived in such-and-such a town..." Aunt Catherine would wave her head and sigh, "That man Walter Briard!" and clam up. I had a vaporish idea why she disapproved of him. It had to do with the word "moral" and what he did for a living and the way we lived.

I'm not sure there is an accurate term to describe what my father did professionally. "Art-objects-investor-dealer-junkshop-keeper" might be near. Or "one-man-mobile-Tiffany & Company-Bettman Archives-Wildenstein Gallery-and any side-street antique-shop" could be nearer. For "father's occupation" on the entrance forms Ben and I brought home one of the times we entered a new school, my father wrote "merchant." But he was in a whimsical mood, not yet being able to look seriously upon our academic careers. Actually, he had a multitudinous collection of priceless paintings, sculptures, books, gems, and mediocre artifacts that had attracted him during his affluent, roaming young manhood. And at this time in his life, he was engaged in selling these things, piece by piece, for very high prices indeed, to carefully sought clients who happened to reside in widely distant communities across America. Major sales required weeks—in some cases, months—of his personal consultation. And so naturally, Ben, Fred, and I went with him.

We never lived in a hotel. My father despised them, having spent so much of his life in them. We thought of our recurrent upheavals as "moving." A day would come every so often—always a surprise day—and a crew of bulky men would arrive and pack up everything we owned, except my father's velvet-lined satchel of precious stones. That, my father allowed Ben to carry to the car. Fred oversaw the entire operation like a harried, but very polite, credit manager, and then happily donned his chauffeur's cap and took the wheel of our black, seven-passenger Buick. And we would precede the vans, bulging with household effects and merchandise, to our destination. Sometimes we would have enough room there for all the stuff. But most times, living room chair space was yielded for crates of Dresden china and Danish glassware and stacks of original editions supported by ornate silver candlesticks and clocks and gilt-framed nudes and landscapes and Chinese flowers. We lived in old, large houses with dozens of dim, badly placed cupboards and in small houses with no closets at all, in dry houses and leaky ones, ones on hilltops and ones in valleys. Some my father rented, others he borrowed. Occasionally, he bought one to resell it later. A few times, because a friend or client talked persuasively of his own projects, after many drinks and conferences with architects, a house was designed just for us. Those always sported a curved staircase with niches at various heights along it for my father's favorite pieces of sculpture—the ones he didn't intend to sell.

Aunt Catherine saw all this as a haphazard, nomadic, and certainly unhealthy life that was bound to produce criminal offspring (Ben and me) or, at best, adults even more strange than our father.

Our father did not extend himself for us in the customary American sense. He didn't play games with us. He didn't have any interest in what we ate—we ate what he ate. It didn't occur to him to buy a baseball for Ben or a doll for me. He never took us to kiddie-lands. He simply shared with us whatever entertained him. He read to us from Tolstoy, Shakespeare, Cervantes, and Chaucer (my name, Lucresse, came out of *The Legend of Good Women*). He took us to regular adult movies and to operas in New York and to plays and museums all over the nation, to foreign restaurants and to the magnificent imitations of European tourist sites that were the homes of his clients. Still, Aunt Catherine's dark suspicions were not completely invalid.

The photograph album of my memory is monotonous: First, me—skinny, stringy-haired at various ages, but always pale with fear—standing in front of some strange woman's desk, offering a progressively dirtier, more cluttered card of transfer. Then, me—in a party dress, hostess at a birthday party—smiling emphatically into the half circle of my small guests, whose faces I had seen once before in my life. My father's recipe for blending us quickly into each community was to throw a birthday party for Ben or me, and invite our whole class the day after we joined it. Some years Ben and I celebrated as many as four birthdays apiece.

I can see my father now at these affairs. In his early sixties, he was a heavy, solid man with all his own beautiful, even teeth, though his face was deeply lined. He had thick, white hair that somehow refused to stay combed, and he wore suits that had been made twenty years before to last for twenty-five. They didn't look shabby, just a little too big for him. He would stand against a wall, behind the table of paper-hatted children, with his hands fidgeting behind his broad back. He remained each time, silent and smiling, for only a short interval, until after Fred, with tears shimmering behind his glasses, carried in the antique silver tray with cake. Party after party, on Fred's arrival, our newest acquaintances burst into song, and Ben or I truly believed for the musical moment that this was our natal day, and these were our lifelong pals. And, what with the rubbery social code that governs childhood relationships, the guests did become our staunch friends and enemies for the ensuing weeks.

In a way, we owed all of these relationships to Aunt Catherine. At least I did; Ben was gregarious enough to find his place in the neighborhood gang within hours after we explored each of our latest quarters. It was Catherine who pressured my father into letting us attend school in the first place. Public school—private too, for that matter—was among a number of popular causes he did not believe in for us. My father had been instructed by tutors, and when I was five and a half and Ben nearly seven, he engaged one for us. The young man was extraordinarily handsome, in a passionate Sicilian manner, a dedicated artist who wanted to earn his keep while painting nudes. My father turned the skylighted upstairs hallway of that particular house into a studio-bedroom, and got his protégé a morning job in a local gas station. Every morning, Fred, wearing his beloved chauffeur's cap, drove the young man to work and called for him at noon. After lunch, Ben and I trailed him up to his studio, where he let us feel his muscles and watch him mix colors. He set large pieces of drawing paper on the floor for us and tested his mixtures on them, making big, startling letters for us to copy. For years after, in my mind, *A* had to be fiery orange, *B* a sad misty blue, and *C* a spirited green.

Aunt Catherine's visit that year occurred a couple of weeks into our lessons—we were up to weathered-gray *U*. After kibitzing one of our sessions, she decided that we were learning little else but the anatomy of the human body, a subject in which we were already more than sufficiently instructed, she felt. She was doubly shocked to hear that this constituted Ben's first formal educating experience and she initiated a shrill campaign to get my father to send us both to regular school. He met it with tranquil, heedless smiles and soft reminders that Hui Tsung, Caesar, Cellini, Buddha, and Jesus Christ had never attended academic institutions.

Ben was thrilled with the idea, even though it had come from Aunt Catherine, and I acted favorably disposed to it too, to be a member of the majority. Our nagging campaign was reinforced by Aunt Catherine's weekly letters marked "Important" assuring my father that in twentieth-century America, a "decent" education for the young was compulsory by law, and that if he persisted in denying one to his own flesh and blood, it would be her patriotic duty to report his negligence and irresponsibility to the "proper authorities."

The following September, our handsome tutor found a studio elsewhere, and Ben and I began—me in the first grade, Ben in the second—our pilgrimages to the brick shrines of elementary learning.

To this day, at half a block, I can detect the salty, musty odor of chalk-dust, child-dirt, disinfected washrooms, steamy gymnasiums, and hot-soup cafeterias; in a very few years we spent time in approximately eighteen sources of this odor, and in an effort to make each new one "mine" as fast as possible, I perfected my own technique for instant blending—a supplement to my father's opening-party maneuver: I lied. This got me noticed and, at its most effective, admired with dispatch.

In one rusted-brick building, outside of Detroit, I confided to an eager, but slow, boy in my second-grade class that one of my eyes was false. I wouldn't say which one, and I glowed for the remaining weeks we were there at the interested, curious stares from the desks near mine. On the playground of a brick structure in Macon, Georgia, I told a yellow-headed little girl that I was really a twenty-three-year-old midget—surely she must have guessed having seen at my birthday party how old my *father* was? In one of my third grades, near Topeka, where I learned to count to twenty in French without knowing from the teacher's flat Midwestern accent that it was the same language my father spoke fluently and Ben and I understood haltingly, a sizable clique looked upon me with terrified envy. Its members had been led to believe that I was actually two people, only one of which they could see, the other being an invisible witch who carried a poisoned comb at all times. My visible personality won enormous respect...*that* Lucresse was courageous and kindly, to keep the other Lucresse from killing off everybody with a sudden vicious touch of her comb.

In Providence, Rhode Island, I picked a credulous, motherly-type little girl to tell that I was in secret communication with Ghostland. I was sort of a queen to its inhabitants. They adored me from afar and wept over my messages and longed for me to come rule over them. My confidante assumed that my family belonged to some weird religious cult. And, knowing my father's antipathy to all organized religious bodies, I was compelled to threaten that I'd make a child-Ghostlander of her with a wallop on her head if she repeated that derisive assumption. I never used that lie again.

But then it was always more rewarding to think up new ones, test one set of lies against another on different audiences, dispensing with a control group. My timing was fairly good; we nearly always moved before boredom, sophistication, or a more potent attraction eclipsed my magnificence. I was found out and exposed only once and, ironically, that experience, which provoked a virtual earthquake in the foundations of deceit upon which my happiness was built, began when I told the truth.

Wally Noonan, a stocky boy with squinty eyes, whose father was second assistant foreman of the local fire department, had been bedded with the measles when we settled in his town in northern Texas. Wally was the only one of my new fourth-grade classmates to miss my ice-breaking and cake-cutting party—my third that year. By the time he recuperated and came back to school, I was pretty well established. I had dispersed the information that I walked in my sleep (unhappily, that *had* occurred for several nights running after each of our last four moves) and that you could stick pins in me and I didn't wake up. (Not so. Ben, into whose room I usually walked, gave me a punch on the shoulder that unfailingly woke me, causing me to flail in all directions in furious retaliation.) Also, I had released my most elaborate story to date, to a mousey little girl who had a "best friend" who was cruelly extroverted and friendly with practically every other little girl in the class. I whispered that my brother and I, and a sister, had been welded together before our birth. Ben was bigger than I was since our sister and I were so weak from fighting with him to get free, that when we had broken off, we had to be stuffed back into our mother for another year and a half. After that interlude, we started to wiggle out again, but my sister proved to be still too weak, and by this time, so was our mother. Tragically, they had both perished during the struggle. I could just barely remember how they had screamed and prayed—in some mysterious gypsy dialect—as they died. With rounded eyes, my timid new friend said how "luck, luck, lucky" my brother and I had been to have survived such a terrible ordeal.

The Friday that Wally Noonan recovered from the measles and returned to his desk, in front of mine, we were studying about money. I was finding the problems very difficult, not having had the preparatory lessons in fractions and percentages. The teacher, Miss Lyle, asked me three questions that morning, and I answered all three with a puzzled, suffering silence. Wally, one of the quickest arithmeticians in the class, was openly contemptuous. During recess, when he found that others were willing to forgive my ignorance because of my remarkable history—someone told him about my sleepwalking—he was downright angry.

"Most mothers don't want nobody to know they got a crazy kid that walks around asleep," he said, squinting at me with dark, resentful pupils. "You shouldn't talk so much."

"I don't have a mother," I countered.

"You don't *know* much either. You don't even know how many cents is in a dollar."

"That might be 'cause she's part of triplets," my withdrawn little chum offered from the sidelines.

"Triplets!" Wally was intimidated by the credulity on the surrounding faces. "Well, so what? She still don't know nothin' 'bout *money*!"

All the children looked at me to brace their wavering certainty about my tragic history.

"I do so know about money." Not entirely untrue as I had heard my father mention figures occasionally, usually in the hundreds and thousands. Money was something I guessed he had a great deal of, and that I'd never been the least interested in, until that moment. With my heart jolting me, I said, "I may not know about *parts* of money. But I know about great, big, huge amounts of it. There's a painting over my bed that cost four thousand dollars."

Wally let out a disbelieving "Haw!" and the others, except for my mousey friend, followed suit and moved away snickering the good-natured, disdainful snickers of in-the-know folk who are too smart to be fooled.

Two relevant things happened that afternoon. Miss Lyle announced that the annual class spelling bee would be held the following Tuesday after school, and that we should invite our parents to it; and Aunt Catherine, having arrived midday for once, was there when I got home. "Jen would be so happy to know we're together," she was saying to my father when I burst in.

My father called Fred and told him to bring a highball for him and a cup of tea for Aunt Catherine.

"Didn't the painting over my bed cost four thousand dollars?" I demanded.

"What?" said Aunt Catherine.

"No," said my father. "Seven. It cost *me* four. I sold it last week. Which reminds me, I wonder when that chap means to pick it up. I never did like it very much. But why did you ask?"

"I wonder too," said Aunt Catherine, looking at me the way she did when she suspected that I had a fever.

"No reason," I said and escaped.

The following Sunday morning, my father personally awakened Ben and me early. "You are going to church," he announced. "Today. In half an hour."

"Why?" we whined, astonished.

Fred had taken us a few times, to whichever one was nearest, professing each time that we were going for a short drive. It was a standing joke between him and my father—that he had put one over on Mr. Briard.

But this time, my father was proposing it. "Think what a nice surprise it'll be for your aunt when she gets up," he said.

We dashed into our clothes. The joke was being turned on Aunt Catherine! She, who deprived herself of going to worship when she was at our house, as she couldn't take us without a good deal of discussion, was to discover that the infidels were more godly than she was this Sabbath!

Fred drove us, to the Methodists' edifice this time, and let us out. He had to get back to serve Aunt Catherine's breakfast. She loved everything about that—the silver coffee pot, Fred's little bow when he poured for her from it, the broad exaggeration of his normal, slightly Welsh accent that he used to satisfy her notion of British speech.

"Now go in and mind your manners," he said to us. "I'll come fetch you at twelve."

Ben and I looked in, feeling the tenor of the place. I saw only one face I knew. Wally Noonan was edging into a pew between two young grownups. He spied me at the same time I saw him and pantomimed his scornful "Haw!"

"I'm not going in."

"I don't want to either," Ben responded, for reasons that I was willing to leave unexplored.

We walked around to the back steps of the church, facing the congregation's private cemetery, and sat down. For a while we practiced belching, and then we argued about which end of a piece of spaghetti was the beginning. After that, we argued about the way people pronounced the word "here" in Pennsylvania and North Carolina. And then we got on to the subject of what we wanted to do when we grew up.

"I definitely want to be an actor," Ben declared. "I decided yesterday."

I couldn't think of anything I wanted to be or do. "I'll probably just get older and bigger and die."

Then, staring at the acre of gravestones glinting in the sun in front of us, we talked about death, concluding that it wasn't so bad. When you were dead, you didn't know you were dead. And then, though we didn't say so, we both thought of our mother, who neither of us could remember, and all of a sudden we were holding hands. We sat there like that, sorry and wondering, in that odd, compatible way, for several minutes before we got embarrassed.

"I think you should play Juliet," Ben said suddenly.

Not this again, I thought. I had been violently opposed to this every time he'd persuaded me before—to play Juliet in his own wild version of Shakespeare's romantic tragedy. Every few weeks he'd get a yen to be Mercutio, and go slinging around a twig for a sword. He'd play all the roles himself, except for the titular ones; he'd make Fred and me do those. Our father was always the audience. I, the one sorehead, always put up a vehement battle. In my opinion, Juliet was hopelessly stupid—to knife herself over anybody as unromantic looking as our hairless, bespectacled Fred.

This time Ben's proposition was more imprecatory than ever before. He wanted to do the play with all of us in Chinese makeup, which he had practiced applying recently with yellow chalk and burnt matches. I was categorically refusing when there was a babble of voices from the front of the church—people were coming out. So we abandoned our quarrel and ran around front to look for Fred. He wasn't there yet, so we waited, jumping on and off the curb.

"Hey, are you her brother?" snarled Wally, emerging from the church ahead of his parents.

"Yes," Ben admitted with slight disgust.

"You older than her?"

"Of course."

"Then you're not twins, are you?"

"Of course not," Ben said, from Olympian heights of effrontery.

"You were never triplets either then, *were* you?"

Just then, Fred pulled up and we scurried into the car, Ben laughing and shouting over his shoulder, "It's a good thing *you're* not triplets, lamebrain! So long!"

I didn't try to explain Wally's questioning on the way home. I just said that I knew him, that he was in my class, and that *I* thought he was loony, *too*. Also, that I would play Juliet in Chinese makeup after all, if Ben still wanted me to.

Aunt Catherine exuded approval on our return. We had been communing with her intimate friend, the Lord. And Fred had, probably at my father's suggestion, brought back the current issues of three ladies' magazines, and presented them with her coffee. Her good humor didn't evaporate even when Ben sprang his news about becoming an actor. But I was never more miserable. For the rest of the day—even while mincing about as the Oriental Juliet—I worried about how I could disprove Wally's verbal proof that I was not a triplet.

Late that night, awake in bed, I concluded that I couldn't. Yet, humiliation was a feeling I could not endure. Since the triplets story couldn't be recalled, and neither could any of the others that were probably now also open to doubt, I would have to reinstate my veracity some other way. Wretched, without a single idea, I fell asleep: perchance to dream—or walk.

The next morning in school, Wally's adamant expression made it plain that he didn't intend to allow me expiation. When Miss Lyle left the classroom, trusting us on our honor not to look up from our arithmetic workbooks, he muttered, "Triplets!"

I didn't answer.

"Walking asleep!" he hissed.

The muffled giggling around me melted my insides, but still I kept quiet.

"Painting that cost four thousand dollars...haw, haw, haw!" he said right out loud.

"It cost seven now," I squeaked.

At this, the whole class unloosed the happy whoops that had been choking them, and Miss Lyle returned at a gallop with a tranquilizing dirty look at me—how did she know?

"Enough!" she declared, distributing sheets of paper from a pile she had just fetched. "You'll see I've given you each a list of the hundred words we've learned this semester. Many of them—maybe all—will be asked in the spelling bee tomorrow. You may take your lists home and refresh your memories this evening so that you'll all have an equal chance of winning." She smiled and recommended again that we invite our parents. There would be punch and cookies in the cafeteria afterward, and a new five-dollar bill would be awarded to the winner.

The last announcement drew titillated "Mmms!" and "Oh boys!" and at dismissal, the chatter revolved around the glorious prize and speculations about what each aspirant would buy if he won: a case of Dr Peppers, a BB gun, a Bob Wills and His Texas Playboys Banjo. One girl even said a share of Mid-Continent Oil Co. stock. Clearly, the winner was going to be a hero or a heroine.

I caught Wally's arm as he was leaving the cloakroom. "I am going to win the spelling bee," I said.

For an instant he looked dumb, as though paralyzed, then he recovered. "Haw!" He broke away.

"I am too going to win!" I hollered after him for all to hear. "You'll see!" Clutching my word sheet with all my might, I started to cry. I cried all the way home.

It took fifteen minutes on my father's lap, a fourteen-ounce glass of iced tea (to which he would have added a thimbleful of scotch, I knew, had Aunt Catherine not been there), the expulsion of Ben from the house, and the first harsh words I'd ever heard my father say to Aunt Catherine, who, in response to my emotional hurricane had just remarked that I seemed unhappy, to hear the words necessary to console me.

"Catherine," snapped my father, "you are gifted with astounding powers of observation!"

Chastised, Aunt Catherine controlled her compassion and remained silent as I explained about the spelling bee and the absolute necessity of my winning it.

"In that case," my father said, unwrinkling my wadded word sheet, "we must see that you know all these words. But tell me, why do you absolutely *have* to win?"

"Because I said I would and that's got to be the *truth*."

"And why does that 'got' to be the truth?" he said, slower and lower.

Aunt Catherine shook her head despairingly at the conclusive evidence that Walter Briard didn't value the truth as much as she did. Fred seated himself, in readiness for a lengthy session. And I began to sob again.

"Because I lie and they know it!" I wailed. "I told the biggest lie I ever told."

"You told *what*?" gasped Aunt Catherine.

"A lie. *L-I-E*! And Wally Noonan found *out* it was a lie and *told* them all it was a lie!"

Lie, lie, lie. At the repetitive confession, Aunt Catherine mouthed the word in horror, her hands leaping to her temples, pointy elbows at right angles to her head. She resembled a modern dancer projecting distress to the last row in the balcony, or a penguin in an animated cartoon. She could no more inhibit the gesture than I could my tears, but she earned a scathing glance from my father for it, and she left the room murmuring, "Poor Jen...poor Jen."

Remarkably, my hysteria seemed to depart with her. I blew my nose with finality, and my father dumped me off his lap. "Now, not that it matters much," he said, "but we can't help being curious. What *was* the lie you were caught perpetrating?"

In answer, I recounted the entire saga of the triplets.

"Implausible," he remarked when I was finished. And we all burst out laughing.

Then we got down to work on the immediate problem, the word list. We quickly discovered that I knew how to spell most of the words on it, although I didn't know how I knew. There were only about fifteen whose construction was unfathomable to me, and those we reviewed over and over. By dinnertime, I had memorized nearly *all* of them successfully enough to shout back their spellings a split-second after being given the words. Only two, "cupboard" and "believe," continued to stump me. My mind developed an immovable block against them. After being corrected ten times, "cupboard" still came out minus its *P* and the *I-E* sequence in "believe" remained inverted. After dinner, we went over the words again. And again I missed them as often as I got them right.

"It isn't likely that you'll be asked these particular two anyway," my father said. "So don't worry. Get to bed. And remember, Fred and I will be there to give you moral support."

At the time, I didn't realize what a brave promise that was for my father to make—what misgivings he must have anticipated. He was as sensitive as Aunt Catherine (from an altogether disparate set of principles, of course) to his position as an aging father of motherless young children. And he was as uncomfortable at any gathering of usual parents and youngsters, especially in schools, as she would have been at a dice table. This was why he stood in the shadows at our birthday parties, why he delegated Fred to enroll us in new schools, why he rarely set foot in them unless his presence was essential. This time he felt it was, and he must have steeled his courage for the task.

Wishing me good-night, he promised again, twice, "Don't worry, Fred and I will be there. We'll be there."

"But don't let *her* come," I said, knowing he'd like to hear it.

"I won't," he assured me tenderly. "Sleep well, dearest Lucresse."

Indeed, the next day the two men sitting among the other parents in the rows of chairs set up for the occasion *did* seem like a pair of ancient classics misplaced on a shelf of best-selling paperback thrillers. From the place I took at one end of the line of my classmates in the front of the room, hoping Miss Lyle would begin the questioning at the other end, I saw their white and bald heads nod to me, and a recrudescent lie almost escaped me—remarking to the girl on my right that those were my two grandfathers. But the girl had been to my party and had seen them before, so I forced it back and tried to concentrate on what some of the words on the list had been. My hands were sticky and cold, and I couldn't remember one.

The twitter died down and Miss Lyle said, "All right, we'll begin with you, Lucresse. 'Pound.'"

Though that was one of the words I'd known right off, I went into a state of open-mouthed shock—at the monumental error in my calculations. *Why on earth did I stand at this end of the line?*

"'Pound,' Lucresse," repeated Miss Lyle, smiling encouragingly.

"You mean the 'hit' kind or the 'weight' kind?" I blurted.

A general laugh broke out and I could see my father and Fred glance about them, openly hostile. How desperately I regretted not somehow keeping them from coming.

"Either kind," said Miss Lyle, smothering her own amusement.

"Oh," I said loftily, unwilling to be grateful, and I spelled the word faultlessly.

Miss Lyle continued down the line, eliminating ten of the twenty-five of us. Mentally, I spelled correctly all the words asked, except "ocean" and "cupboard." This time, in my mind, I left out "cupboard's" *B*. I passed my next turn with ease, on "basket," the next with "charge," and only four of us remained. Wally Noonan had left the ranks on the previous round, dragging his feet. He now sat with his good-sport parents, glaring at me. Two more turns passed and two of my quartet were counted out. Only I and a quiet, bony boy I had never spoken to were left. I stared at my feet to avoid Wally's undeviating gaze as well as the embarrassingly happy faces my father and Fred presented now, while my partner spelled "circus" without a hitch. Then it was my turn again.

"'Believe,'" Miss Lyle said distinctly.

Convulsively, I began. "*B-E-*" in a tone that would dispel any doubt that the word began with those letters. Then, dumbfounded, I stopped. For the life of me, I couldn't remember whether it was *I-E* or *E-I.* I squinted the way Wally did habitually and pretended to look off into space, thinking.

The pause became noticeably long. "Yes?" said Miss Lyle. "*B-E-?*" and my opponent shifted, raptly hopeful.

Movement in the back of the room attracted my eye. Fred, apparently having some sort of mad fit, was pounding the sides of his shiny head with his fists. He did it again and again, with such force that he knocked off his glasses. They went clinking to the floor, and when he bent to retrieve them, to my horror, my father took up the same lunatic behavior. Aghast, I watched, weighing whether I should scream at them, "What's the matter with you?" or turn around and run home as fast as I could and get Aunt Catherine, when all at once the meaning of what they were doing struck me: they were imitating Aunt Catherine's reaction to the word "lie." I gulped and shouted, *"L-I-E-V-E!"*

My opponent was either shaken into forgetfulness by the disappointing drama of my recovery, or as fortune had it, he drew a word he didn't know. "Recess" defeated him on his next turn, and I stood alone, the declared winner.

Out of respect for the truth now—and I still sometimes have as much trouble being faithful to it as anybody else—I don't recall exactly what happened next. Somehow we all got from the classroom to the cafeteria, where I broke away from my father and Fred to accept the more important congratulations of some of my classmates. Wally Noonan approached, on the verge of tears. "My dad is gonna give the prize," he said.

I hadn't known that, but it made sense. Mr. Noonan, being the second assistant foreman of the fire department, was probably the highest-ranking civilian among the parents involved or the town officials available for the honor.

"And I'm gonna tell him not to give it to *you!*" Wally added, his voice breaking, and he dashed off.

In fresh agony, I rejoined my father and Fred and waited. Any moment Mr. Noonan might explain to the assembly what Wally must have noticed, that I had been aided with "believe."

I watched as he listened briefly to his son, then motioned to him to stand aside with his mother. He exchanged a handshake with Miss Lyle and then asked Lucresse Briard to please come forward.

I stood before him, staring straight ahead so hard that the buttons on his suit coat began to look as big as saucers. I didn't hear what he said and didn't know what he was doing, until I felt the sharp edge of the crisp paper on my hand. Then everyone clapped dutifully, except Wally.

"See him?" I said a little later to my father in the hubbub of departing. "That's Wally Noonan, the one that said I lied. He said he wouldn't let his father give me the prize, too." I started to giggle.

"Quid pro quo," my father said.

I didn't know what that meant, but something about the way he said it made me stop giggling.

It wasn't until three or four weeks later, during our drive to San Francisco a day ahead of the vans, that he used the phrase again, and Ben asked for a translation. "Tit for tat," my father explained, giving me a conspiratorial smile.

But by that time the phrase held no disquieting impact for me. I had gotten rid of the five-dollar bill by presenting it to Aunt Catherine as a good-bye gift when she left for Sapulpa the day after the spelling bee. She was reluctant to accept it at first, but eventually did. She stuck it neatly into the zippered compartment of her black pocketbook, her sharp eyes wet with tears. "I'll use it to buy flowers for Jen's grave."

CHAPTER TWO: DEBUTS

Everybody knows that San Francisco is distinguished by its hills and hotels and bridges.

But San Francisco is distinguished to me because Aunt Catherine didn't visit us there, because Ben and I were in the same class there, because Ben made his first public theatrical appearance there, because Fred almost left our employ there, and because of Miss Narcissa Bunce.

We lived there in what we ever afterward referred to as "the leaky house." It was a small, weather-stained cedar affair that listed carelessly to the east on the crest of a west-bent rise, a position that allowed it to store water in mysterious pockets between its sloping roof and off-level ceilings and disperse it in constant rhythmic drip-drops for days after a rain subsided.

Our school there, a mile across the indigenous hills, was brick again and harbored the same hot smells and disciplined fidgeting we'd become familiar with. And, we soon realized, when Ben and I and our transfer cards arrived in its principal's office, its board of education was operating within—well within—a particularly stringent budget.

Our records showed, wornly but still clearly, that Ben had been attending the fifth grade, and I the fourth. This caused the lady-principal considerable concern. The fourth grade (evidently due to an inexplicable hyperprocreative impulse rampant thereabouts nine years before) was hopelessly overpopulated. One more pupil would endanger the potential education of all the others. The principal's forehead-wiping worry made me uncomfortable, and Fred had already left for home.

"I won't take up much room," I said, "and since I'm not especially anxious to be educated anyway, I won't take up hardly any of the teacher's time."

But the woman was adamant. The *fifth* grade was *not* filled to capacity, she said, fingering her hairline. "We'll see how well you do in the fifth grade with Ben."

To make her feel better about it—there was no way of making Ben feel better—I said that my upgrading was probably right because I was having a birthday party the following Saturday.

She rechecked the data on my softened transfer card. "But you were nine last month," she replied, perturbed.

Under the circumstances, Ben was more loyal than I would have predicted. "She said she was having a birthday *party* Saturday, not a *birthday,*" he explained benevolently.

"Oh." She wiped her forehead again, and we were directed to our newest homeroom.

We soon found another reason to suspect that the budget was limited. All activities other than basic reading, spelling, history, arithmetic, and embryonic science instruction were under the aegis of one person...Miss Bunce. She was recognized only as "Music Teacher," but due to funds, the theory that if you know anything about one of the arts, you know everything about 'em all, was in full practice. She was in screaming charge of first- to-sixth-grade art exhibiting, square dancing, glee clubbing, assembly programming, beginning instrumental instruction, and dramatic productions.

She was a towering, tense woman with a small head, a resounding voice, and huge hands, which she used with hammering fervor at her upright piano—its top even with her spasm-ridden eyebrows. And at the moment of our matriculation, she was inextricably, despairingly involved in the creation of a self-concocted operetta called *Flowers of Spring* that was to be the exchange program with San Bruno's elementary school three weeks hence.

Ben saw the situation as luck-sent, supplying a vehicle to test his abilities before a larger audience than Fred, my father, and me. The second day, during Miss Bunce's regular singing instruction session with our class, he raised his hand six times to inquire about the forthcoming production. He had doubts that "Welcome, Sweet Springtime" was exactly right for the opening. He thought perhaps it would be better sung by a soloist. He thought Miss Bunce ought not to fill the role of introducer of the numbers, that that role could be expanded to include short narratives between the scheduled songs and recitations. He wondered why all the fifth-grade girls were required to sing. Couldn't most of them just stand around and look all right in their blue bell costumes, and let only those who *could* sing, sing—perhaps as accompaniment to a soloist?

Ben's only difficulty in attaining the role of narrator-soloist was that, after three days, Miss Bunce couldn't stand him. She made that clear in the middle of another of his suggestions by pounding out a murderous minor ninth and commenting, "We got along pretty well without you until now, Ben Briard, so will you please keep quiet and just be a good leaf?"

All fifth-grade boys were reluctantly (for other reasons than Ben's) blooming alto leaves. To Ben, fluttering anonymously as one of them, when he envisioned himself as an imposing tree, was a searing manifestation of Miss Bunce's heinous, heedless lack of appreciation.

Climbing the hill home that afternoon, he complained. "Those kids can't sing. *You* heard them. And how do you think they'll sound without *her* right in front of them, directing? Terrible, that's how. Worse. And she knows it—that's why she's always screaming at them."

"Isn't she going to *be* directing them, from the piano, at San Bruno's?"

"No, stupid. You never listen. In the auditorium there, the piano's down on the floor, in front. They're going to be up on the *stage*. Of course, I guess she *has* to play the piano part..." His face stopped, stunned with pleasure. "Except if she got somebody else to play it."

"Who?" I asked.

"You, for instance."

"Me? But I'm a blue bell!"

"But you're not making it any better by being a blue bell. And she's wasting me on a leaf," he retorted. "If you could play the piano for the whole thing, she could lead all those dumb blue bells and leaves. And maybe she'd see how important that was, and let somebody else do the introductions."

"But, Ben, I can't play a piano."

"How do you know until you try? She could teach you to play the accompaniment. It looks easy. And you'd be helping her out. She likes you. Then, if you offer to help her, she'll like you even more. And she'll like me too, because we're related. See?"

"Ben, I don't think she likes me. I don't think she knows I'm there."

"You've got to make her know it, but not the way I did. You've got to keep her liking you. Will you tell her you'll play the piano for the thing or not? Yes or no."

"Well, I'll try."

It was a halfway commitment, but enough of the fraction to make me consider what I might be letting myself in for. I decided that it would be very nice to play the piano for the performance. Ben was so good at many things—this might be something I'd be good at. And it did look easy.

At the next day's singing session, Miss Bunce banged a key chord and yelled, "Now, your best voices!"

Best was synonymous with loudest.

"Just a song at twi-li-ight—when the lights are lo-o-ow—and the flick'ring shad-dows—softly come and go-oo—," we bellowed.

"Hold it! Stop!" Miss Bunce shouted, smashing out a thunderous discord. "Lucresse Briard! What are you doing in the front row! You don't sit there!"

"I traded with *her*," I said, indicating the girl named Janet in the seat behind mine.

Janet whispered, "She's a skunk."

I didn't know whether she meant me or Miss Bunce, but it didn't matter; I had to secure this position.

"I wanted to be able to see you better, Miss Bunce," I said.

"Hee-hee," came sotto voce from Janet.

"Good girl," came a ventriloquist-like rasp from Ben in the back row of the boys' section.

"I think you can see me from anywhere in this room."

"I mean your fingers. I'm learning to play the piano."

"Oh—well, that's very nice, Lucresse. I guess it's all right if you sit there, as long as you pay attention to our songs too."

"I will. I really will."

"It's all right with you, isn't it, Janet?" Miss Bunce said.

"Oh, sure. It really is," Janet agreed, sticking the toe of one shoe through the open back of my chair.

After the last bell that afternoon, I dashed back to Miss Bunce's room and offered to stack the songbooks for her. She let me. I asked her if she studied music when she was nine. She said yes. I told her I hoped I'd be as tall as she was when I grew up and that her hands were beautiful. She looked at me with mild, not displeased, surprise.

"Is there anything else I can do for you?" I asked.

"No. Just don't squirm in class while the leaves sing 'Welcome, Sweet Springtime.'"

"I won't," I promised, and I could hear my breath going in and out.

"But there *is* something else I can do for you, Miss Bunce. I can play the piano for the singing while you lead, if you just show me how."

Her head jerked up nearer the ceiling. "Show you *how*?"

"Oh, I'm sure I can play—it's just that I don't know *what* yet, if you see what I mean," I said reassuringly.

Probably from a reasonable urge to get rid of me as promptly and kindly as possible and get home, she suggested that I play something for her.

I sat down before the orderly keys, my hands in my lap. I was in no rush. I judged it would take her at least an hour to teach me all I needed to know to beat the keys into ringing sound the way she did. "What shall I play?" I asked. "Which ones?"

"You mean, which *keys*?" she said, her voice catching. Then she smiled. "All right, Lucresse. Play C-sharp."

"What?"

"Lucresse, you haven't had piano lessons, have you?"

"Not until now."

"Don't you see? If you want to play the piano, you need *instruction*."

"Yes. Sure." I thoroughly agreed. "So I can play the accompaniment and you can lead the singing better."

"Now, Lucresse, what I'm trying to tell you is that we don't give piano instruction in the public school system. Do you have a piano at home?"

"No," I said desperately.

"I see," she said, examining my suffering eyes, my dress, my good shoes, and doubtless reckoning that my family, like most families enduring the recent downturn of the economy, was forfeiting other pleasures to clothe me so well. "There *is* instruction in the trombone and trumpet, starting in the sixth grade. Why don't you wait until next year and study one of those instruments?"

Not only did I not wish to explain that I had reason to believe I wouldn't be in the sixth grade in this school's system, but I was now overwhelmed with desire to play on the provocative keyboard.

"But I don't want to play something you blow," I said, trying to cry. "I want to play the piano—now—so I can play it for the program. I want to the way Ben wants to do the introductions and sing 'Welcome, Sweet Springtime' by himself."

"Oh he does, does he?"

"And he can—if you'll let him. And *I* can—if you'll show me how."

She turned her pinched face skyward. "Why is it I can't get the people I *need* to work this way?" she asked heaven. "The mothers on the costume committee, for example. The leotards came from the factory last Tuesday, but only the Lord knows if the wardrobe the ladies are supposed to be making will be ready on time."

I ceased urging the tears that wouldn't come. "Miss Bunce, if you'll let Ben do the introducing and the talking and the singing he wants, and teach me to play the accompaniment, we'll get the costumes done for you—all of them."

"Listen, Lucresse," she said wearily, "I have no doubt Ben could do the narrative, and sing some songs, alone. I don't even doubt that you could learn to play a few decent chords, if you had a piano at home, which you don't. But how do you think you and Ben can finish twenty blue bells' costumes—with ruffled headpieces—in seventeen days? Tell me that."

"It wouldn't be just Ben and me. There's somebody who lives with us who knows how to sew."

"Who would be willing to finish twenty costumes?"

"Sure. This person would do anything for Ben and me."

She smiled again, sort of an envious, admiring smile, and I presumed her acceptance of the deal. "And I can get a piano at home, too," I added. "That's nothing to worry about. Now, will you tell me where C-sharp is?"

She pulled a chair next to mine and sat down. "Now, pay attention," she said in a businesslike tone. She put my right hand in a five-finger position on the keys, her own in the same position further up. "Your thumb—your first finger from now on—is on middle C. The black one above it is C-sharp. My first finger is on C, too—not middle C—just the C two octaves up."

She showed me that all the keys had names and how those names were indicated by written notes on staffs, in measures, on paper, and that you don't fall from one to the other of them on the instrument; you keep your wrist level with your elbow and your knuckles up, and you hit each one with independent hammer motions of the fingers. She showed me the fingering of a complete scale for each hand, what flats and sharps and a natural and a chord were. She explained I'd have to practice hard. "I have a beginner's book somewhere," she said.

I tried several timid tonic thirds and an even braver, falling apart arpeggio, while she flapped through a stack of worn paper-covered bindings on a book shelf. "Here. You work from this at home, and if you come to something you don't understand, you can ask me about it after school." The lesson was obviously over. "But not later than three forty-five," she added, looking at her wristwatch.

"Oh, *thank* you." I clasped the book.

"You'd better check with that person who'll do anything for you about doing the blue bells' costumes," she said, locking her desk and getting her car keys out of her handbag.

I trotted at her hip to her car. "I'm sure it's all right about the costumes. Can I tell Ben you'll let him do the you-know-what?"

"If you can learn to play 'The Blue Bells of Scotland' by next Wednesday," she said, and drove off. That the Scottish air had to do with a war-deprived lovelorn maiden rather than with flowers had not deprived Miss Bunce from scheduling its performance by the blue bells of the fifth grade.

When I got home, I didn't think once of informing Fred of the forthcoming emergent need for his seamstress service; the issue of how I was to acquire a piano was of such preeminence. I exploded with the request.

My father warmed to the idea immediately. The client he had moved to San Francisco to see had a magnificent pianoforte, a seventeenth-century one, if he could persuade the fellow to sell it.

"Oh, please *don't*," Fred begged, considering the additional specialist moving men such a purchase would necessitate.

"But it's a beautiful thing," my father insisted.

"No, Mr. Briard."

"But, Fred," I interjected, "If I don't get a piano right away, Ben has to stay a *leaf*."

My father had, as usual, an attitude of hands-off sympathy for Ben's ambition, but his arguing for the piano was motivated more by desire for another art treasure.

"You haven't *seen* this piano," he said acerbically to Fred. "It's inlaid with—"

"No. Absolutely no, sir," Fred insisted.

"I cannot see your reasoning," my father rebutted.

"Mr. Briard, I've said nothing in all these years about the two Empress beds you found necessary for Lucresse, because they were such a beautiful pair, or those enormous bronze plant holders that won't hold a daisy, but are so beautiful—but we do not have space for a beautiful piano!"

"Couldn't we get one that's *not* beautiful?" Ben suggested.

My father could do no more than gesture his disgust at such an idea, but to me it had real merit.

"One that we could leave here when we move?" I said hopefully. "I only need it for two-and-a-half weeks."

Fred, at military attention, stated his position with ultimatum clarity. "I will agree to a small, cheap, ugly piano that we can abandon.

Should a beautiful seventeenth-century piano be carried into this already overweighted leaky house, I will move out and go back across the seas from whence I came."

"If you get a cheap, ugly piano, dear children, you will get it by yourselves," my father said bitterly. "I will have nothing to do with it."

"Will you pay for it?" I asked.

"You *will* pay for it?" asked Ben, more positively.

"No more than twenty-five dollars. And if it's ugly, it's not worth that."

"Thank him for his unsparing generosity, children," said Fred, squinting nastily through his spectacles at my father. "I'll try to help you find an inexpensive piano, but I doubt that there is one *so* inexpensive in the entire western half of the United States. If you need twenty-five dollars more, *I* shall provide it, with all my good wishes."

"Oh, Fred!" I said, hugging him—as much to make my father feel bad as to make Fred feel good. "But you're already going to have enough to do for us, what with the twenty costumes."

"What costumes?" Fred unclasped my arms from his waist.

"For the blue bells," I said, and I explained my bargain with Miss Bunce.

"Ho-ho!" my father exclaimed.

Fred removed his glasses and breathed on them furiously. "How *could* you promise such a thing, Lucresse? A few buttons, surely—but twenty costumes? No. Definitely, no!"

"But if you don't," Ben pleaded, "I won't get to do anything but be another leaf. Why make *me* suffer? *I* didn't promise you'd do the costumes. It's all Lucresse's fault."

"It was your idea for me to play the piano," I retaliated.

Fred snapped his glasses back on behind his ears. "At the rate I sew, it would take me the fortnight, without sleep, to do up twenty costumes. No, young sir, and no to you, mum. I have enough to do."

"Please, Fred?" Ben and I pleaded.

"Why, Fred, what's happened to your compassion?" my father teased. "Take pity on these poor, corrupt little beggars."

"Great heavens above, I need strength to control myself. All right, Mr. Briard—being it is as it is—I'll make my own bargain with you. *All* of you. I do not withdraw my offer to help pay for a cheap piano, but I will *not* help find one. And I will not take one blasted stitch in one blasted costume unless all of you share the work of making all twenty. I can teach you to sew as well as I. If that isn't a satisfactory bargain, I will prepare my notice on the spot."

"If you made that threat more than once every ten years, I'd take you up on it," my father said. "Now, we accept your bargain."

"Agreed. Children, just let me know when you need the money."

I asked Ben twice, in my father's hearing, how one goes about buying a cheap piano. Both times Ben said he had to think about it, and my father just went on silently doing whatever he was doing at his jumbled desk. Late in the afternoon, when I thought Fred might be in a better mood, I tried him. Though calm, he said, "I declared I wouldn't help, and I'm a man of my word."

Even later, when I judged that my father may have softened to a call for help—he was reading the evening newspaper and appeared to be far removed from the realities in his immediate household, and therefore more easily persuaded to face them with detachment—I brought up the subject again, in a louder than necessary voice.

"Ben, *how* can we find a piano? Where?"

The paper didn't move from its position in front of my father's face.

"I'm still thinking about it," Ben said.

My voice grew louder. "But the book Miss Bunce gave me to learn from has sixty-four pages, and I only have seventeen days."

Without moving the newspaper so that we could see his face, my father said, very low, "When you want something, you have to let other people know."

"We *have* let you and Fred know," I said indignantly.

"You have to let *other* people know, people who may have cheap pianos that they wish to sell," the voice spoke from behind the paper.

"But we don't know who the people *are* who have cheap pianos and want to sell them," Ben said.

"You have to *find* them, dig them out, separate them from all the people who *don't* have cheap, ugly pianos for sale."

I felt like punching the newspaper. "How?" I said desperately.

"You'll have to deduce the answer for that yourself. I'm busy reading a notice about an auction in Marin where I may pick up one of the tapestries Mr. William Randolph Hearst missed."

Ben was no more intelligent than I. His intelligence was, characteristically, just put to use more quickly than mine.

"May we see that newspaper when you're through?" he asked politely.

"You may, if you don't construe this as aid or report it to Fred."

A moment later, with me at his shoulder, Ben found a column headed, "Merchandise For Sale." One two-line ad caught our fast and slow intelligence. Ben read it aloud. "Piano. Uprt. Chp." The address was on a business street on the way to our school. The ad was signed "A. Forelli."

My father suggested that I stop in to see Mr. Forelli in the morning, but Ben could not come with me because "Nobody, not even Ben, should influence my decision whether or not to buy a cheap, ugly piano." The responsibility was to be mine alone.

The next morning, Ben left me at the address—a recently opened dry-cleaning shop; Mr. Forelli was its proprietor.

"Avanti, Avanti," he said. "Your mamma, she send a little girl to look first? C'mon, it's in the back."

The instrument had a muddy-brown, scarred case and chipped, yellowing keys. Its top was higher than Miss Bunce's piano's, and its backboard was nicked around the pedals. In large, gold Gothic lettering above the keyboard, "Needham" was printed, and beneath that, "New York."

"You see?" said Mr. Forelli, "She's American."

To the right of Needham and New York was the designation, "Upright Concert Grand." I didn't ask what that meant and Mr. Forelli didn't say.

"You know Milano?" he asked. "The shoemaker had this store before? He liked music, so he had this here. When he die, his wife, she say she ain't payin' to move it out...I can have it. But I don't want it. So he liked music? So why couldn't he listen to the radio like me?"

From under a pressing table, he pulled a dusty bench over for me. Even with my fledgling instruction, I detected that you could almost blow the keys down. And Mr. Milano either hadn't liked B-flats or at some time he'd mistakenly engaged a plumber to repair all eight. Not one of them sounded.

"You tell your mamma she can have it for twenty dollari if she take it away," Mr. Forelli said.

"And how much would it cost to move it?"

"Ah, now I see why she send a little girl! You live near?"

"Yes."

"Then, I tell you what. If she want it, my boy and me, we put it on my delivery truck and bring it. But it still twenty dollari. After all, I paid for the paper ad."

"We want it, all right. You bring it," I said. "Today."

"*Calma!* We ask your mamma first, eh?"

"My *father* said it would be all right. He'll pay you the twenty dollars."

When I came home from school the next day, the piano was in my room, hidden from my father's critical sight. I wouldn't let Fred dust it or Ben touch it. I only suffered everyone to listen to it. It and Miss Bunce's book became the focal points of my existence. To an audience that didn't even try to conceal its displeasure, all that afternoon and evening I practiced beginning exercises and scales, less their B-flats. I played them for Miss Bunce the next afternoon, and she used the principal's telephone to arrange for one of the more willing members of the reprehensible costume committee to deliver the unfinished costumes to our house that very evening.

The next week was filled with fulfilling our various bargains. Fred, tight-lipped and antagonistic, directed sewing sessions. He was particularly abusive about my father's difficulty with mastering the craft of tacking a light material to a heavier host, the veiled headpieces. My father spent one entire session searching for a silver thimble that he'd once bought as a gift for me but had forgotten to give me. Now he used it himself, and that, added to his missing one work period, compounded Fred's anger. He invented opportunities to remind my father that he was hardly abiding by the bargain. In return, my father kept reminding Fred that his grandiose gesture of offering Ben and me financial aid had not been called to action. Ben bent to the sewing task with intense, distracted grace, his mind chained to the purpose of memorizing the introductions and lyrics to "Welcome, Sweet Springtime." The only waking hours we ceased sewing, practicing, memorizing, and complaining were the afternoon my birthday party came and went.

Three days before the exchange program, the costumes were finished. My father was criticizing Fred's handiwork and musing that he himself might have become a very successful tailor. Ben could do the introductions and "Welcome, Sweet Springtime" in his sleep, and I could play "The Blue Bells of Scotland" and the chord progressions Miss Bunce had arranged as accompaniment for her bedecked vocalists.

Last rehearsals were wars of sound: Miss Bunce's larynx, frantically urging the chorus to shriller and shriller heights, pitted against me stabbing the keys with all my might, and Ben's lone, melodic greeting spring "in so-ong" contesting unscheduled noise from the restless leaves and blue bells.

The night before the performance, Ben said his throat hurt. My father looked at it and said it couldn't. Ben said his stomach ached. My father said it would stop.

"*Flowers of Spring* is going to be awful. Those kids don't know what they're doing. I wouldn't come see it if I were you."

"But you and Lucresse are in it. And I've contributed more needlework than ten women. Certainly Fred and I will be there."

"Tell him how awful it's going to be, Lucresse," Ben ordered.

I didn't know if I should support him or not. "Are the other parents going?"

"Sure. But what difference does it make? The point is, it's going to be awful."

It made all the difference to me. My father and Fred would again be the odd, conspicuous old among the usual young.

"Don't come. Please don't," I begged. "You and Fred already heard Ben do his part, and you've heard me."

"You'll make Lucresse nervous," Ben added.

The prospect of the performance had not made me nervous, until now. Now, instantly, I translated the strange, strained behavior I'd noticed in many of my friends in their parents' presence. They were nervous. Mothers were overly interested in their daughters being ladylike; I was glad I didn't have that situation. Fathers with young, unsure faces were so anxious to be proud of their sons. Regardless of whether my father hoped for me to be ladylike, regardless of whether he wanted me to make him proud, I wanted to be like the others. I would be nervous if he came.

"Yes, it would make me nervous," I said.

"Tomorrow at two thirty will never happen again," my father said. "And you both know that. You're going to do something you'll never do again. Of course you'll both be nervous—but you'll do the best you can. And I wouldn't miss it for anything."

"Suppose something goes wrong and I'm out there all by myself?" Ben said.

"Nothing ever goes completely right."

Ben woke up in the morning sniffling and speaking in a new, echoey voice. "I've got a cold. I've got the worst cold adybody ever had!"

He attributed it to a new breakthrough in the ceiling above his bed which silently dripped cold water onto his pillow all night.

"What ki'd of crazy house *is* this adyhow?" he said.

My father looked hurt.

I came to my father's defense. "Aw, Ben, we've lived in worser ones."

"Worse," my father corrected.

"No, we haven't," Fred interjected.

"A'd I have to si'g!" Ben wailed.

Fred had seen us through chicken pox, measles, and mumps. Immediately, he gave Ben his own adjunct to any medicine a doctor ever prescribed, a cup of boiling hot coffee with a tablespoonful of whiskey stirred in. He was convinced that heat and alcohol could cure any disease. This time they relieved the congestion in Ben's nose and left his eyes glazed, his muscles relaxed, and his voice more resonant. Fred was pleased. "I'll bring you some more in a thermos before the performance," he assured Ben.

An adult seeing Miss Bunce lurching around in the schoolyard as she frenziedly herded us all into the buses hired to take us to San Bruno might have suspected that she too had swallowed a few bracers in preparation for the occasion. No doubt she hadn't; it was her unfamiliar high-heels causing the imbalance.

At San Bruno, I went with her and the blue bells to a classroom where they were to change into their costumes. It took a half hour to snap and hook fast all their leotards, another half hour to adjust all our creations over them, and twenty minutes more to attach headpieces. The whole process could have taken twenty minutes had not Miss Bunce been scolding one child after another, and had not one of the interested mothers been flitting about resnapping snaps that she was sure hadn't been securely snapped in the first place and telling every girl she looked "adorable."

Fifteen minutes before curtain time, we met the leaves and Ben, who had been ensconced in a different classroom, on the stage. Miss Bunce bounced across it screeching between clenched teeth, "Everybody ready?" The children took turns teasing and tugging each other away from the curtains' center where they could peek out. Hysteria built as waves of hostility floated up to us from our audience, composed mostly of our San Bruno fourth- and fifth-grade counterparts, glad that they weren't in our places and waiting to see how badly we'd do.

Ben coughed in everyone's face and warned, "Keep real quiet while I'm singing, or else."

I pulled his arm. "Ben! I think I've forgotten the tra-la part of 'Flowers that Bloom in the Spring'!"

"You *got* to remember!" he said, shaking a fist at me.

"Now, now, Ben—" Fred's voice said, as he came to us from the wings, carrying a thermos. "You mustn't treat Lucresse that way. Here. Sip this."

"Quiet! Everybody get ready!" Miss Bunce hissed, teetering above a babbling cluster of net-covered heads. "Quiet!"

"Quiet!" Ben repeated, in a startling unconscious imitation of her normal bugle voice.

There was a sudden silence onstage, making the chattering from the auditorium more deafening.

"Take your positions, everybody," Miss Bunce ordered.

In one continuous motion, Ben drained the steaming, doctored coffee, shoved the thermos back at Fred, and leapt to a statue-stance where the curtains met.

"I do hope you don't catch his cold," Fred whispered to me and hurried away through the wings.

Miss Bunce and I left the lined-up blue bells and leaves and went out front to the piano by the same route Fred had taken. I sat next to her on the bench as she got ready to strike the opening chord cue for Ben's solo rendition of "Welcome, Sweet Springtime," and I tried not to see my father and Fred in the third row amidst the San Bruno youngsters and the San Francisco parents who'd made the trek for the event. The two men looked even older and more enthusiastic than I'd feared.

Miss Bunce struck the chord and left her fingers resting on the keyboard. The center of the curtain jutted and yanked about, but didn't part to reveal Ben and the company. She struck the chord again and stepped on the sustaining pedal. Still, the curtains didn't open. The silence, which had come gradually over the auditorium, was broken by beginning murmurs.

"Run in and find out what's happening," Miss Bunce whispered between violent breaths.

I sprinted. Backstage, boredom and bedlam reigned with equal strength. The bored few stood shifting about in their approximate places. The bedlam was caused by all the others, who seemed to be rushing back and forth from the stage to the exit to the hall on the other side, pulling and yanking at their costumes. The formerly flattering young mother-aide was dashing from escapee to escapee, rehooking and resnapping with vicious might. Ben, holding the center of the curtains in a deathlike grip, was inquiring desperately over his shoulder of one and all, "What's the matter? Why isn't everybody in place?"

I approached the quietest songstress—ordinarily a bystander type. "What's happening?"

"Janet had to go to the bathroom," she whispered.

"But what about everybody else?"

She shrugged. "They all had to go too, I guess."

The delay was understandable. The bathroom was situated a third of a block down the hall, and satisfaction of this sudden mass urge was not possible with the snapped and hooked costumes and leotards in place. Complete undressing and redressing for the number of people milling in and out could take an hour.

I ran to Ben with the information.

"Why can't they hold it?" he said at me, as though I, not Janet, had set off the chain reaction. "If I wanted to, I could go too, but...never mind. Tell Miss Bunce I'm coming out to do 'Welcome' in three minutes, whether they're ready or not. Go on. I'll count to sixty just three times."

He reminded me of my father: absolute purpose untouched by practicality, a firm belief that it was worth trying to order things as one wanted them to be, no matter what the odds or consequences.

I hurried back out to Miss Bunce to give her the news. "Oh my gracious!" she muttered, sending the now boisterous audience a twitching deceitful smile over my head. "Just wait till I get my hands on them."

From the way she was kneading her hands in her lap, I was happy I wasn't a blue bell.

A spotlight shone on the middle of the stage's apron. Ben parted the curtains enough to slide through, and there he was, his eyes shining at the noisy throng. Miss Bunce struck her chord again, but to no avail. The intemperate babbling grew louder, if anything.

Ben put his hands on his hips, threw back his head, and shouted, "Quiet!"

There was laughter, a few boos, and some joyous applause from the vicinity of the third row. I lowered my eyes so as not to confirm the identity of the isolated claque.

"I'm going to sing whether you hear me or not!" Ben yelled.

That earned a burst of laughter. Then, as Miss Bunce, seemingly in a trance now, banged out the key chord once more, awful, total silence.

Ben's head wobbled from side to side before finding a relaxed, balanced position on his neck. A slow, beatific smile spread across his face. "Now you are ready," he complimented his audience. "I am Ben Briard, and our program is called *Flowers of Spring*. I will open it by singing 'Welcome, Sweet Springtime,' accompanied by our director, Miss Narcissa Bunce, down there at the piano. The girl next to her is Lucresse Briard and she'll play the accompaniment for the rest of the program." He included Miss Bunce and me in his gracious smile for all the world. We stared dumbly at him.

Clapping came from the third row again and was duplicated in dots from other rows. Miss Bunce hit her chord for the last time, and Ben sailed into song.

He sang it better than he had in practice. The cold and the coffee made his voice more carrying and less strained. And having an audience of strangers had an electric effect on him. When he held the last note as long as possible, it occurred to me that he didn't want to end the song. Ben would like to stay up there alone in the light as long as he lived. But it had to end, and the second it was over, even before the applause broke, Miss Bunce shoved my music in front of hers and galloped away backstage.

Ben took three bows, the last one and a half unnecessary, in my opinion, and I braced my fingers for "The Flowers that Bloom in the Spring." Reluctantly, Ben withdrew through the curtain, the blissful smile lingering softly on his lips as he disappeared.

My fingers trembled waiting for the curtains to draw aside, revealing the revelers. My fingers began to ache.

The middle curtain shook and Ben returned. As I watched him, wide-eyed, he said, "There will be a short delay because some members of the cast are not quite ready...because...they're not. Lucresse Briard will play 'The Blue Bells of Scotland.'"

Immediately there was a terrible clapping from the third row. I dared to glance its way and almost tumbled off the piano bench as I saw hundreds of pairs of eyes looking straight and expectantly into mine.

I looked to Ben for reassurance, but he was no longer there. I placed my hands in the familiar position of the opening notes, and as if they weren't attached to me, much less under my control, they began to move. They played measure after measure, and most of them sounded unfamiliar, out of tune, discordant, though my fingering was automatic and accurate. It wasn't until the closing chord, when I took a good look at them, that I realized I had played the entire piece in a different key from the one it was written in.

Ben returned, applauding with the audience. I was tempted to stand up and bow as he had before, but I was afraid my legs wouldn't hold me.

I prepared for the opening of "Flowers that Bloom" again and waited for him to announce the number.

"Will you play something else for us, Lucresse?" he inquired smoothly.

"NO!" I croaked, in shock.

"Well, ladies and gentlemen," said Ben with barely a pause, "this isn't really part of the program, but they're still not ready back there, and Miss Bunce said something had to be done, so I'm going to do something. It's part of a play named *Romeo and Juliet* by a man named Shakespeare. He lived a real long time ago in the ancient times and he wrote a lot of swell stuff, only you need a whole bunch of actors to do a lot of it, except if you don't have them and then you can act out swell parts by yourself like this one. You'll see what I mean.

"I'm Mercutio, a real brave character that just got stabbed and is about to die, but his stupid friend—the dumb Romeo who the play's named for—he says the hurt can't be so bad. And I say, 'No, 'tis not so deep as a well, nor so wide as a church door..."

Ben acted it up, clutching at the general area of his heart and lurching from foot to foot. At the end, as he collapsed, a boy in a back row yelled, "Say, he's some crazy kid, ain't he!" Others stamped their feet and whistled and some took up the cry, "More! Do some more!"

Ben jumped to his feet and hollered back, "Sure!"

Miss Bunce's furious face poked out from between the curtains behind him. The mouth moved and the face was quickly withdrawn. Ben held up his hands, the glad stamina going out of his body. "The program is finally ready," he announced. "I'm sorry."

The curtains parted all the way, exposing the most terrified group of faces, including Miss Bunce's, I've ever seen.

"They'll sing 'The Flowers that Bloom in the Spring,'" Ben said, and stalked off into the wings.

Miss Bunce raised her hands, and the wooden faces and my wooden hands did their duty, song after song.

Between the songs, the applause was loudest when Ben came out to make the introductions.

At the very end, Miss Bunce gestured to me to join them on the stage. Before I could get to her side, Ben hurried out from the wings to her side to share the curtain call. As I joined them, the lights made me squint and my feet felt foolish.

"We will sing 'My Country 'Tis of Thee,'" Miss Bunce announced, digging her heels into the stage floor. "You are invited to join in."

She about-turned, stopping herself with her heels again, and Ben began the song, in his own most comfortable key. Miss Bunce, I, the leaves and blue bells, and the audience went into "sweet land of liberty" in the same key.

As "Le-et free-dom ring," died out, I heard a burst of laughter that was all too familiar. My father.

"I wonder what *he* thinks is so funny," Miss Bunce remarked as the curtains swept closed in front of us.

Ben and I let her get embroiled with the mob, and we made our way down to the auditorium, where my father was still laughing. All his top teeth were showing; there were tears glittering in his eyes.

"You both did very well," he explained, "but Fred almost caused an international incident here."

"Yes, you did very well indeed," Fred said quickly. "Jolly good."

"When everyone else sang 'Let freedom ring,'" my father choked back laughter, "Fred rang out, 'God Save the Queen'! He's rarely been in such fine voice."

My father and Fred drove us back to our school, trailing the buses filled with our classmates and Miss Bunce. In the schoolyard, Fred said innocently, "You ought to go in with the children, don't you think, Mr. Briard? To compliment Miss Bunce. She worked so well with Ben and Lucresse."

It was my father's turn to be embarrassed. "That's her business," he said abruptly.

The inside of our car was the closest he got to the inside of our San Francisco school.

The next day, Ben's cold was gone. A note, in tiny, delicate handwriting, incongruous with her physiognomy, came to Mrs. Walter Briard from Miss Bunce, thanking her for her fine contribution to the costume committee and saying that Ben and I were a fine pair of youngsters and that she thought the program went off fine. She told our class the program could have been better, and it wasn't mentioned again until the day, two months later, that Ben and I picked up our further handled transfer cards.

When she heard we were leaving, Miss Bunce said she'd be thinking of us the next time they had an exchange program and she bid us good luck. And at the end of our last school day, Janet, who had become one of my closest friends and whom Ben ignored since the occasion of her stampede-instigating bathroom break, stopped me in the corridor. "I didn't want to tell you before," she said, "but at the end of the program when you came up on stage, I could see right through your dress. And my mother says she just despises kids that show off, like your brother."

CHAPTER THREE: SEXUAL STIRRINGS

We left the upright concert grand in the leaky house, and Ben deliberately explained to the empty-eyed old woman in charge of the admissions office at our next school that I rightfully belonged back in the fourth grade. That was mean and foolish of him, because, in that school—between Hulbert and Edmondson in Arkansas (my father's client had a holiday ranch across the border outside of Memphis)—it wouldn't have mattered which grade I was in. Every class had boys and girls, with queer haircuts and queerer speech habits, as old as seventeen.

There was one general store that also housed the post office and the one-man police-fire–chief's headquarters. Marijuana grew under its back windows. The older boys in my class picked it on their way to Sunday school, the Sabbath being the only day that the police officer wouldn't catch them since he went to the church earlier than they, being the Sunday school teacher, too.

We didn't stay there long. Fred offended the storekeeper to the point of open enmity by asking the last name of his young, black helper and thereafter addressing the fellow as "Mr." My father took to correcting my English almost every time I opened my mouth. Ben got embroiled in a ferocious argument with a fifteen-year-old boy in his class over whether boxing was an art or a science; I don't know which side Ben represented, but he came home with a cut lip. And his opponent, continuing the fracas, stole our car that night. The police chief recovered it and confiscated it as evidence for a week. It was certainly useful evidence. We saw him drive past our house in it on his way to his office every morning.

Even Aunt Catherine, who visited us there for a long weekend, didn't think this town the ideal place for us to settle down—not that she had any real hope that we would settle anywhere. The "community life" appeared to her to be limited compared to Sapulpa's; there was no Kiwanis club for my father.

He sold whatever it was he wanted to sell to his Tennessee client without prolonged negotiation, and we left. For Macon, Georgia, I think. But I'm not positive.

As bread lines lengthened around the country and construction came to a shrieking halt, my father's trade in priceless art objects remained strangely unaffected, and our life plodded on. Ben perfected his imitations of Bing Crosby and both Nelson Eddy and Jeanette McDonald. As a comfortable child among children with unemployed parents, I continued to feel on the outside of whatever life we were inhabiting. And Fred dealt with our constant upheavals by developing his own unique cause, to which he devoted insistent energy—even threatening to strike. He was determined to persuade my father to have dinner at the same time every evening. True to his character, my father never did succumb to regularity, and Fred never did strike.

In the year I was twelve and Ben was thirteen, I refused to have boys to my birthday party and Ben wouldn't invite girls to his. Our attitudes died hard. The last party we had, before insisting that we were too old for such celebrations, was a double production when I was nearing thirteen. I invited only girls and he only boys. The sexes giggled at and insulted each other and had a fine time. Then suddenly

Ben and I were a lot taller, though still straight and narrow-bodied, and we were fourteen and fifteen, and on our way to Palm Beach, Florida.

Ordinarily when we moved, neither Ben nor I, nor Fred, knew the specific reason. We were used to people floating in and out of our lives and long-distance phone calls that led us to pick up and move someplace else.

The move to Palm Beach was different. Perhaps I was more interested than before in the exact nature of our propelling force. My father was excited. He had been commissioned by a jewelry firm in New York to buy the Peddicord diamond for them. And the Peddicord diamond, one of the largest in the world, belonged to Mrs. Mead Peddicord, Jr., who was in Palm Beach at the time.

Mrs. Peddicord, Jr., better known as the motion picture actress Felicity Gorham, had so far resisted every offer of purchase.

This presented a challenge my father found titillating. He enjoyed the flattery implicit in the New York company appointing him to achieve by personal contact what they couldn't, as much as he liked the prospect of the fee agreed upon for his successful service, a small percentage of the gem's value, a sum close to $100,000. I've never known a more tumultuous winter.

The house my father was able to buy by remote decision through an agent was unimpressive. Bright, blond stucco on the outside, dim, pocked plaster inside, vaguely Spanish, with mosaic-tile floors. But it was adequate to house us and our goods. The goods, as usual, hung around and leaned around wherever space offered itself. And we each had a room—my father, two. Fred's was belatedly built—an addition to the garage reached via a staircase off the kitchen. Ben's and mine were off the second-floor hall and shared a bathroom situated between them. My father had a duplicate of our layout off the opposite side of the hall.

Felicity Gorham, from what the butcher told Fred and some refound, old acquaintances told my father, was in a seafront mansion. Once we were there, he didn't look her up right away. He seemed to be in no hurry. After a few weeks—time enough for Ben to become his tenth-grade speech teacher's favorite and for me to become familiar with my ninth-grade homeroom teacher's right name (it was Wyatt, and I kept getting it confused with a Wyle and a Wyant I'd once had)—when he'd still made no attempt to meet her, he met her by accident, through Ben and me.

On weekends and occasionally after school, we had swimming lessons at the pool of one of the most elaborate resort hotels. After each lesson, I liked to linger in the calm water no higher than my chin and pretend to perform an accomplished crawl. Ben's instruction had been more fruitful. He preferred to practice his stroke and unfearful breathing in the more turbulent ocean. There was a daily argument as to whether we'd go to the beach or the pool. Usually my father settled the dispute by taking me to the pool, where, after one swim back and forth, he donned a robe and sat at a table on the surrounding patio nodding approval of my efforts as he sipped a highball. And he permitted Ben to go to the beach, so long as he was with friends, or, if friends weren't available, Fred.

I couldn't understand why, when friends weren't available, Ben accepted Fred's company without protest—until the first time I was compelled to go to the beach too because my father was keeping an appointment with a young architect whose ideas for a small, modern house near the shore interested him temporarily.

Fred considered exposure of the skin to direct sunrays uncivilized. Once, years before, at Brighton, when he had evidently already become bald, he had lain for only twenty minutes, he said, unshielded from a summer sun, and had to salve every inch of his fair-complexioned, so mistreated body, including his tortured skull, every hour on the hour for two weeks with a vile-smelling, medicated slime. Now he was unshakable in his distrust of tropical sun, his dislike of sand, and his repulsion to moving salt water.

To accompany Ben and me to a place replete with these abominations, Fred geared himself with a long-sleeved shirt, Bermuda shorts, high socks, a wide-brimmed straw hat, a jar of Noxzema, one blanket, and three bed sheets. Ben and I carried our own towels. At the edge of the pavement where the sand shore began, Fred removed his shoes, wrapped one sheet, Moslem style around his waist, making sure it skirted his legs to his toes. He laid another sheet, half-unfolded, over the top of his hat, and warning us not to step on crabs or shells, hobbled and hopped in the soft, despicable sand to the nearest spot he could get us to encamp. There, he spread the blanket flat and covered it with the last sheet, in hopes of barring the entrance of the powderiest grain of sand through his floor, and he sat down in the very center of his tiny stronghold of civilization, cross-legged, with his Noxzema jar in his lap. He unfurled the sheet balanced on his hat and draped it from its middle fold over his entire person, like a tent. He then arranged the smallest possible aperture, no more than the width of his glasses, between the sheet's meeting edges, as a sighting spot from which he could fulfill his duty as potential rescuer of human life from the vicious ocean.

When he thought Ben was out too far—beyond the nearest breaker—(I gave him no cause for that worry), he poked a shrouded arm upward, making a pointed knob in his tent. For every five times I thought Ben was too far out, Fred's signal went up only once. So most of the time the temptation to close his sighting gap and shelter the bridge of his nose must have won out over his sense of duty, which explained Ben's passive attitude about having him along.

It was I who was waving wildly to Ben to come in closer when Felicity Gorham entered our lives. She appeared at my side from somewhere way down the beach. Ben was bobbing up and down, and from shore, you couldn't tell if his open mouth was joyous or desperate.

"What the devil is that dope doing?" she said in a voice almost as low as Ben's, when his didn't break in a girlish squeak that had been causing him severe anguish.

"I guess he's all right," I said. "He's my brother."

When I turned to look at her, my first impression was of movement—an illusion created by color and wind, since she was standing still, one hand on her hip. She was wearing a white, feathery one-piece bathing suit; the breeze blew its soft, fuzzy surface this way and that. Her hair, blowing above, was a startling halo, each individual hair a brilliant, sundown gold, not one casting a shadow on another. A ring on the fourth finger of her hand at her hip did a patter dance of its own as it caught the sun. It was a rectangular diamond that reached from her knuckle almost to the middle joint and made you think it must take effort for her to lift her hand.

Her eyes were very round and large and deep brown, incongruous with her dazzling hair. And her nose was another surprise—unusually thin, a perfect concave curve from bridge to tip. It was a controlled, fragile, questioning nose, at odds with the personality her bathing suit, hair, and voice described. I turned back to Ben.

"I don't want to *call* him," I said. "I don't want to get Fred up. He's supposed to be watching us." I indicated the sheet-tent thirty yards away.

"That's *somebody*?" she asked.

"Our father's man. He hates the sun."

"Well, I'll call the kid. What's his name?"

"Ben."

She held out her left arm, the unweighted one, parallel to her shoulder, and with a commanding sweep, brought it past her full bosom to her right shoulder, calling at the same time in a voice that was a worthy adversary to the ocean's roar, "C'mon in, Ben!" and added, under her breath, "Damn it."

Fred's curtains sprang apart, knocking off his hat. He risked broiling his skull for a moment. "Ben? Ben? Ben, come *out*!"

Ben surged up, cognizant of us all, and without another bounce, his head moved closer and closer. Fred recovered his hat and retrenched.

Ben approached us, smiling. "I was having a good time," he said to my companion. He planted himself in front of us, standing abnormally straight in the constantly wetted sand.

"Who could tell?" said Felicity, smiling back at him. She seemed to know and appreciate instantly the image of himself he was offering for her approval. "Even the champeens don't fool around that far out in the ocean."

"Sorry if I frightened you." Ben didn't look sorry about anything in this world. I was glad for him that it all came out in one register. "I'm Ben Briard," he continued. "She's Lucresse—my sister."

"She told me."

"I know who you are. Felicity Gorham."

"Mrs. Mead Peddicord," she corrected.

"I've seen you in the movies."

"Yes." She was suddenly bored.

I didn't remember seeing her in any movie. And if Ben had, without me, he hadn't mentioned it before this. It was the name Peddicord, coupled with the blinding gem on her finger, that held my interest now.

"Our father sure would like to meet you," I said.

"Oh my God."

From that, and Ben's tormented face, I knew I'd said the wrong thing. But I couldn't fathom what the right thing might be, to a woman who had that color hair and was famous and wore a ring that was the reason I was trying to remember my homeroom teacher's name.

"Don't tell me your father's president of the Everglades Fan Club?" she said good-humoredly, as though she was afraid she had hurt my feelings.

"No. He doesn't like movies very much." I hoped that would lend him, and me, an aura of sophistication.

"Miss Gorham," Ben began again.

"Mrs. Peddicord," she corrected again. "Mrs. Mead Peddicord, Jr."

"Mrs. Peddicord didn't come to Palm Beach to *meet* people," Ben said to me.

On top of his rebuff, she smiled at me and said, "Thanks, anyway." She didn't want my feelings to be hurt again.

"Can you sit down?" Ben asked. It was a logical question, considering the fit of her wavy-haired bathing suit.

"No. Not here. This suit might decide to curl up and die if it got wet. I only put it on to take a walk down the beach in. I always dress for the occasion."

Ben laughed immoderately. "Go get one of Fred's sheets, Lucresse."

I ran to Fred. "That's Mrs. Peddicord," I told him breathlessly. "The one Daddy has to see."

He peeked out at her with interest. "My word," he said and gave me the sheet wrapped over his legs.

When I came back with it, Ben was saying "...any *one* role, one great role...is there *one* you want to play?"

"*Uh*-uh," she said as I spread the sheet and we all sat down on it. "I don't want to play anything. I'm through with pictures."

"Oh, you're going to do a play!" Ben gifted her with his own preference.

"*I've* never been on the *stage*," she said with surprising vigor.

"You mean you're retiring at your age?"

I thought she was between thirty and thirty-five, which I didn't consider young. Actually, she was thirty-eight.

"I've *been* retired—since the stinkeroo before the last. And that's just dandy with me. No more skin off *my* nose." She laughed and Ben did too, though I could tell he didn't see what was funny any more than I did.

"I don't think I'll ever retire," he said. "I'm going to be an actor, you know."

"Now, I know."

"When I'm too old for leads, I'll play character roles. Some of the greatest roles are character roles."

"Is that right?" she said, smiling an easy warm smile that had a touch of pity in it. It was the first of countless times that I imagined that Ben was younger than I. He didn't understand her smile, and she knew he didn't.

"Our father isn't retired, and he's sixty-eight," I said, thinking out loud. "But then, he didn't start working until he was forty-five."

"Honest?" she said. Her big eyes had the same round naïveté as some of my earlier confidantes' at my tall tales.

"Our mother's dead," I volunteered.

Any other time I'd told that to a grown-up, I'd felt that I should sound sad about it. But strangely, this woman gave me the feeling that you could tell her anything, just the way it was. "But she didn't die from *work*," I continued. "It was from something wrong with her uterus, after she had me."

"Lucresse, for God's sake," Ben reprimanded.

I ignored him. He had tried with every word to hold her interest, and now, for reasons I didn't know, I had it all. She looked fascinated.

She said, "And you don't feel *guilty* about it? You don't feel *wrong* all the time?"

"No...just most of the time. But not about *that*. She would've died if she had somebody else instead of *me*, or Ben and me."

"Lucresse!" Ben warned.

"Lucresse, you are wonderful, absolutely wonderful," Felicity said.

I loved her.

"You must have a wonderful father."

"Well...he's pretty old."

"Lucresse, gol-ly!" Ben pleaded.

"Tell me, why does he want to meet me? The truth."

Ben and I became dumb. We didn't want to put this striking new acquaintance on a commercial basis. Finally, Ben spoke. "It's sort of a business deal."

"He wants to get *you* started in pictures?"

"Oh, no," Ben said.

"What does your father do?"

I recalled one of the titles he'd once used. "He's a merchant."

"Then he wants to sell me something."

"Oh, no," Ben said.

"So what's the big mystery? You're sure it's me he wants to meet?"

"Yes," I said. "Why don't you come home with us and find out all about it?" I wanted to be around when she and he got together. "Come for dinner."

She laughed a throaty laugh. "Thanks for the invite, but I couldn't possibly."

It occurred to me that if she was "Mrs." Peddicord, there must be a "Mr." She might even have children, back at the mansion.

"Your husband could come too," I urged.

She coughed. "No, Lucresse. He's not here. I'm here for both of us." She stood up. "Tell your father he has a very nice daughter and son, and that I don't want to buy anything. Good-bye."

She was already walking, fast, as Ben and I got to our feet. At fifteen yards, she turned and waved and we waved back.

Ben acted as though her loss was my fault. "You say the damnedest things to people. What makes you think a woman like Felicity Gorham is interested in how old Dad is, and Jen's uterus?"

I folded up Fred's sheet. "She wasn't interested in character acting."

"You just don't know the first thing about people, Lucresse. You act like you're twelve."

We walked together, slowly, to Fred, hating each other.

At home, the feeling grew stronger as we interrupted each other telling my father whom we'd met at the beach. From what Ben reported, he and Mrs. Peddicord could have had a rewarding discussion about the theater, if I hadn't been in the way, barging into their intelligent conversation with unbelievably inane comments. Moreover, he was particularly sorry about my misbehavior because it would make my father's future meeting with her embarrassing, if not impossible. He finished the tirade, "She ended up inviting her to dinner. Of all the gall! Of course Mrs. Peddicord walked away."

"She said I was wonderful."

"She was *acting*, you fool," Ben said.

"I didn't see anything wrong with inviting her to dinner."

"Oh, no, except that was when she ran away."

"But nothing unpleasant happened," my father mused. "And you told her I didn't want to sell her anything...I'm going to call her."

"She already said no," Ben protested.

"I know," my father said.

As he rattled through some papers on his desk looking for the note he had made of her address, I, too, wished he wouldn't call. If Ben was right, I didn't want to see him be cut off, because of me.

In my fourteen-year career of eavesdropping, I hadn't heard anything more interesting to me than his part of that telephone conversation. He started, rather formally, introducing himself and mentioning that she had met Ben and me. There was a short silence, and when he spoke again, his voice was changed. "This *is* Mrs. Peddicord?" he said very seriously. Then his pleasant humor returned. "It was at the beach, not more than an hour ago... You don't have to be sure—I'm sure. Yes, I've often thought they were exceptionally nice people...I wouldn't think of discussing it over the telephone... No, it's extremely important business—to me, not to you. No...no...you're not even warm. No...you may call me Walter. No...this is foolish, Felicity. We must satisfy your curiosity at once. What is it you're drinking?... We have some of that here...I understand that Lucresse invited you to dinner. I'll send Fred for you immediately..." He laughed. "Well, you're going to tonight, Felicity. Now listen carefully. Wash your face and comb your hair and don't drink any more until you get here. Fred will pick you up in twenty minutes. Good-bye, Felicity."

I had tried on four dresses to choose one I believed made me look less skinny, before Fred brought her back. She wore a chiffon gown whose bodice caressed her breasts and whose skirt swirled in a hundred soft folds. It and her silken shoes with sharp heels were the same orange color as her hair. I was impressed that she walked more gracefully on her orange stilts than she had barefoot on the beach, and her eyelashes seemed to have become longer and thicker since we'd met. The ring was still on her fourth finger.

She came in saying, "Hello, Walter Briard. Lucresse. Ben. I should write a book on how to get stoned and sober in twenty minutes. Or, almost sober."

"Then it won't do to continue drinking standing up," my father said, escorting her to the sofa, past the long wall covered with paintings and tapestry and the bookcases and secretary and small, marble-topped tables, all loaded beyond capacity with unrelated objects of my father's collection.

"Where I come from, people put everything away when company's coming," Felicity said. "Looks like you get everything *out*."

She dropped onto the sofa, kicked off her shoes, and tucked her feet under her chiffoned buttocks.

"Where is it that you come from?" my father said, bringing her a drink.

"I'll be damned! First question out of the bag! I could say a lot of places."

"So could I."

Felicity took a full half-inch of her drink in one swallow. "I could say Hollywood. But nobody comes from there. They go there."

"The way they go to hotels."

"The Peddicords come from Short Hills, New Jersey, you know. And I'm Mrs. Mead Peddicord, Jr., yet."

"I know."

She sipped at her glass. "I won't be for long. I'm sitting out the divorce now. The decree comes on November thirtieth. That's a Thursday."

"Oh? I didn't know that," he said.

"So." She took another large swallow. "Where do I come from? You don't know the kick it gives me to tell you. For twenty years you could of killed me before I'd tell." She drained her glass. "I am Frances—only it was 'Fanny'—Goldstein, from the Bronx, New York, One Hundred Sixty-fourth Street. I made it Felicity when I was six, and Felicity Gorham when I was fifteen. I didn't make Peddicord till twenty-seven. That was harder. The move from One Hundred Sixty-fourth Street to Short Hills takes a hell of a lot of work."

My father signaled Ben to refill her glass. "It usually takes two generations, roughly fifty years."

"You can do it by yourself in ten, if you learn how to tell a lot of crumbs how great they are and don't mind having part of your nose cut off."

"If you think that's what you have to do."

"If you think so, so it is," Felicity said. "Now I know why I let you talk me into coming here. I *wanted* to say this out loud to somebody. You see, now I don't give a damn about it and there's nobody to tell. It gets awfully frustrating in that big barn I've got, with nobody to tell. I got to be Mrs. Junior—with this to prove it—" She lifted her hand, wrist up, fingers *U*-ed, to display her ring. "—and all these insights after four years and two months with a psychiatrist and now nobody to let it all out on."

Ben was gazing at her, his opinion confirmed that she was from a different and infinitely superior world. I felt a little troubled, but no less adoring.

"I'm very glad you came," my father said, "for any reason."

"Of course I pretended it was that I wanted to know what you wanted. I guess that's why it took me four years and two months on the couch; I can make myself believe anything, for a while. Incidentally, why *did* you want to see me?"

"I warned you. For commercial purposes. I'm a salesman."

That was a new variation of the "merchant," "businessman," and "antique dealer" that had appeared on my admission cards.

"A salesman of what?" she said.

"Of things. Things you see around here." He gestured to the house in general.

She looked over the room and her eyes stopped on an iron and bronze bell about three inches high that was relegated to silence on top of the secretary. It was a cowbell from Greece that had survived the wagging of Athenian cows for centuries and Fred's wagging in more recent years to call Ben and me in to dinner. It was heavy black and burnt metal, indestructible looking.

"That's kind of interesting," she said. "Bet it makes a hell of a noise."

"It does. But it's not for sale. Nothing here is for sale, to you."

"Walter Briard, what *do* you want?"

"I want to sell something of yours, to someone else, and collect a handsome fee for doing so."

"Like what of mine?" she said slowly.

"You can't guess?"

"No...*uh*-uh."

"You must make directors pull their hair out," he said. "You are a terrible actress, Felicity."

Erupting out of his silence, Ben's voice rang with self-fed wrath at this lightly spoken, but nonetheless—to him—death-dealing invective dealt to Felicity. "That's because in movies, directors don't really work with actors!"

Felicity gave him a kind smile and answered my father. "I couldn't care less if a director has hair or not. I wouldn't care if they all had tulips growing out of their heads. I'm out of that business, for good. So I'm a lousy actress. So to who is that news? So I'm not hot at playing games either. So I don't want to guess what it is you want to sell of mine, Walter."

Her words rattled out faster and faster, more and more in earnest. My knowledge of being drunk was limited to a few movie scenes and Aunt Catherine's censorious opinion of the ingestion of alcohol, but I recognized that Felicity was "under the influence," as Aunt Catherine referred to the condition, and was, by the moment, getting deeper and deeper into it.

She gulped the last drop in her glass, again, and Ben, without a signal from my father, refilled and returned it to her.

"At the same time," she continued, "I want you to tell me what you want to sell of mine."

"That ring you carry around," my father said. "The Peddicord diamond."

"That figures. A couple of months ago, a man from Van Cleef and Arpels tried to buy it from me. He had a bad boil on his neck, but he was more interested in my ring. Now is that normal, I ask you?" Without giving any of us time to reply, she went on. "I said no. Y'see, I was still pretending it was kinda a family heirloom. Now I don't feel that way—but why should I sell it to you? You couldn't want it as much as *I* did when I got it."

"I want it simply because it will give me a great deal of money," my father said. "And I don't know how to live without a great deal of money. I don't need family heirlooms. I could have had all of those I wanted, if I'd wanted them. Instead, I collected a lot of *other* families' heirlooms. Do you understand what I'm saying?"

"Sort of. I've had a fifth by now. Walter...? Walter Briard. You have a beautiful name. Anyhow, what *I'm* saying is, the man with the boil—and another one—he had a sick-looking face, like he knew he wasn't much good anyplace—they didn't have a chance. Because this ring meant something to me more than money. I used up most of my life getting it. Not that Mead would of cared if I'd sold it, any more than he cares now. You know why he married *me*? For just as screwy reasons as I married *him*...because I'd be a freak in his family. He got a charge out of throwing it in their faces that the shapely Miss Goldstein, who had to learn to talk English, was the owner of the diamond that had been in their family for five generations without them ever talking about it. He loved it when I'd do cheesecake shots for the fan magazines with the ring on. He didn't know those shots made my blood crawl as much as his mother's."

"You don't want the ring anymore, do you, Felicity?" my father said.

"I don't know what I want now. I don't need the money. I'll be getting plenty in the divorce. I never needed money, really. My father was manager of the raincoat department in a store downtown until he died. The trouble was he could of owned the store and that wouldn't of made any difference to my mother. She didn't want just a mink coat or to live on Central Park West like her friends. She wanted us all to have been born with a name like Peddicord and her to be sleek and charitable on the society page and me to be presented at court. So nothing he could do or I could do was good enough. Poor woman! The nearest she got to her dream was making a sloppy part-time maid answer the telephone, 'Mrs. Goldstein's residence.' She didn't care if the dust got bushy under the radiators, long as that girl said, 'Mrs. Goldstein's residence.'"

Fred appeared and announced that dinner was served. All through it, I wondered and picked at my food. Felicity devoured hers. Then, sobering, she said, "Walter, give me one good reason why I should sell it to you. I only need one, because you don't have a boil and you're not pale."

"I've already given it to you, Felicity. I want money. If the ring gives you pleasure, then certainly that reason isn't good enough."

"Oh for God's sake, Walter!" she said, shaking her head tempestuously, making her bright hair toss. "Pleasure! The ring's a thing—like Mead. Neither one does anything to me. That funny bell you have out there does more to me. Lucresse does something to me. *You* do. But the ring...?"

"How about me?" Ben asked plaintively.

"You, too," she said without breaking her tempo, "but really, Walter, I thought you knew me better than that."

She stopped, her eyebrows raised in surprise at what she'd said. How well could anyone know anyone else in an hour? Intellectually, the idea that we all knew each other intimately was ridiculous, but, emotionally, we felt it was true. I'd met people my father was fond of saying he had known for "thirty odd years," and I hadn't felt that he knew them as well as we knew Felicity. Also, I had the feeling that the Peddicord diamond had little to do with it and wasn't even important anymore to my father or to her.

"It's just that I have to think about it, Walter. Wanting this stone, and the name that went with it, took up so much of my time. I've changed from the way I was then, but I don't know what I've changed *to* yet."

"You are a lovely person," he said. "There's no hurry about this, Felicity. You can always sell the ring—there'll always be somebody who won't be satisfied until he, or she, gets it. Forget about my offer for now. It will always be there, too."

A tired peace descended on us. For the rest of the meal and afterward, there seemed little need to talk. And when we did, the talk was disconnected and spotty. Felicity lay on her side on the sofa. I sat, feet curled under me as hers had been before, at the other end. My father leaned back in his chair, his legs stretched out and crossed at the ankles. I could see the scraped, worn soles of his shoes. Ben lay on his stomach on the tile floor, reading *Cyrano de Bergerac.*

Felicity and my father each had a snifter of brandy that neither drank with much desire. One of us said something only every now and then, sleepily. I asked her if she had worn lipstick when she was fourteen; she said she wouldn't have been caught dead without it, but that I shouldn't. She asked my father where he had gotten the Greek cowbell; he replied in a small town in southern France, at an auction, where he'd impetuously bought everything being sold. Ben read aloud a speech beginning, "Truly, this passion / Jealous and terrible, which sweeps me on, Is love indeed, with all its mournful madness!" I'd never heard him read it with such whispered conviction. Felicity clapped twice and muttered to an invisible enemy, "Just *try* to sign that boy up, you schlemiel. I got him on a twenty-year contract, if I don't dump him in six months."

She told us about an aunt of hers who'd held it over her family's heads that she lived in "the country"—Flushing, New York—who made peanut butter sandwiches so parsimoniously that you could see the bread through the spread. I told her about Aunt Catherine, who'd never made a sandwich for me, but who always apologized for accepting an average portion of food from Fred's filled platters. My father elaborated that Aunt Catherine was "visiting morality."

Ben offered to read another speech of Cyrano's. I dozed off, and awakened as he was saying, "—I ne'er knew woman's kindness..."

Felicity was face-down, sunk into the sofa, fast asleep. My father's eyes were closed, but his legs were moving, drawing back and stretching outward again. His eyes opened and focused on the mantel clock. "It's ten thirty," he said. "Ben and Lucresse, go to bed."

We went reluctantly. And when we got up in the morning, Felicity was still there, on the sofa, covered with a blanket.

At sometime during the hours I was in school, she returned to the loathed lonely castle she'd rented, packed a suitcase, and returned to our house to occupy the room across the bathroom from my father's. Her title was "house guest."

CHAPTER FOUR: LOVE

We all regarded Felicity's presence as a sensible arrangement; we all wanted to spend a lot of time with her. I regarded it as a wondrous opening-up of my life.

In such proximity, we soon learned that there were several Felicitys. The morning one was sleepy, sweet, slow-talking, anxious that Ben and I ate enough breakfast. She wore silk pajamas and a matching kimono and no makeup. She looked tired and both older and younger than the afternoon and night Felicitys. She spoke in a crooning voice—"Why the hell can't they start schools at a decent time, like noon? I always hated to get up in the morning." Ben and I pleaded with her not to get up when we had to—my father didn't. But she never missed padding down the stairs as we sat down to breakfast and giving us soft kisses on the cheek when we left.

The afternoon Felicity was buoyant, flamboyant, bursting with vitality. It was remarkable how many things she knew how to do, wanted to do, did. With Fred's or Ben's or my cooperation, she scraped all the cracking paint off the iron supports for the staircase rail, taught Fred how to make matzo-ball soup, taught Ben and me how to do a tapping time step and waltz. She taught Ben how to drive the car and both of us how to ride horses. She even succeeded in persuading my father, the nonparticipating audience for most of these activities, to ride with us a few times. His ability to do so astonished Ben and me more than his agreeing to do so, until he explained that though he hadn't ridden in more than three decades, at one time he'd ridden often and quite well. The old wrinkled-leather, but polished, boots, and formal riding habit he unearthed from a long-packed trunk and the relaxed way the inside of his calves gripped the horse testified to his truthfulness. Still, the first time he rode with us, one Sunday dusk, was a happy surprise and lingers in my memory with echoes of the horse hooves on the trail beating rhythm to his words.

"When I was a boy—a hundred years ago—I had a tutor," he told me. "He was my employee and was a friend only of the scholars. I had a father who was my advisor and was a friend only to the figures on his monthly statements; he dealt with money, not people. I had a mother who became one only through the mad, inscrutable ways of nature. She was a friend to institutions, libraries, museums, homes for the homeless; two of them got named for her. My father went to his meetings—fourteen miles to Philadelphia. My mother was carried to her meetings—all meetings were very important—in a carriage, pulled by a horse, of course. In addition to my tutor and the household staff, we housed three carriage horses and, by sheer circumstance, not conscious desire, two saddle horses. *They* were my friends.

"The idea in those days, at least my father's idea, was that a young man of means should see the world, travel, before he came back to settle down for the rest of his life. I never went back. And the only living beings I missed, for a while, were those two saddle horses."

After a moment, Felicity and Ben cantered ahead of us. My father and I were content to keep to a walk. My horse gradually lagged behind his. I shook the reins and slapped his flanks with my ankles, but he refused to catch up.

"Use your heels, Lucresse," my father said, slowing his horse.

I tried it, gently, to no effect.

"Harder. Kick him."

"It won't work. He knows he's bigger than I am."

"But you're smarter than he is. You have to make him know *that*."

I didn't quite see the connection between my brain and my boot, but I angled my foot and swung it full force, knifing the heel edge into the thick horse flesh. The connection between the animal's side and *his* brain, however inferior to mine, became instantly apparent. With the speed of a thunderbolt, he misinterpreted the scope of my order and took off at a gallop. After three dizzying leaps that threw the world and my father suddenly behind me, out of focus, I heard him shout, "Pull on your reins, Lucresse!" Simultaneously, the reins jerked out of my hands, I lost both stirrups, was whirling free in the air, and bumped hard against the invisible, immovable earth.

Next thing I knew, my father was lifting me at my armpits. "Can you stand up?" he asked. "Stand up!"

I was certain my wormy legs wouldn't hold me. And it was deliciously gratifying to have him literally supporting me. This was the first time in a long time that he and I had been alone together. "I feel so weak," I said sorrowfully.

Turning me around to face him, still holding onto my upper arms, he instructed, "Roll your head around."

Languorously, I let my head fall frontward, backward, and to each side.

"Move your arms up and down."

Smiling piteously, I slowly, gracefully lifted and lowered my arms. "I don't suppose they're broken," I said, hoping he was worrying that they were.

With no forewarning, he released my arms. "Walk."

The shock made my startled legs come to life and action. I walked over to a fence post bordering the trail, angry at myself for not having collapsed at his feet.

"All right. Sit down for a minute." He went after our horses that were contentedly nibbling at clumps of weeds nearby. He then hitched them to the post and sat on the sandy trailside next to me.

"It's just part of learning," he said, more philosophical than comforting. "When we get home, take a hot bath."

"Felicity rides very well, doesn't she?" I said after a time.

"She's worked at it."

"Do you think she's beautiful?"

It was not easy to surprise my father. He took the figments of people's imaginations, the infinite variety of weaknesses and deceits and unexpected kindness rampant in humanity as a matter of course. But I could tell my question was a jolt.

"No," he answered with inordinate emphasis. "I don't think Felicity is beautiful."

I was surprised. "She once won a beauty contest. Did you know that?"

"There is no such thing as a beauty contest," he said, vexed. "Beauty is noncompetitive. Beauty of any kind stands alone, unmatched, inimitable, uncontested. Felicity isn't a work of nature, Lucresse. She's a contrived work, shaped by mediocre tastes and much suffering."

He was just talking, or lying to me, I decided, or he was just too old to see Felicity as the girls and particularly the boys I knew, and their younger fathers, would see her. "I think her hair is pretty," I persisted.

"I think it's hideous."

Now he must be joking, I thought. For some patronizing reason, he didn't want me to know how much he admired Felicity's looks, so I gave up trying to make him discuss the subject.

In the distance, Felicity and Ben were riding back to find us.

"Ben hasn't ridden any more than I have," I said. "I wonder why *he* hasn't fallen off."

My father concentrated on Ben trotting toward us. Ben's heels were down, his hands low and quiet. He was sitting to the trot. In pace with him, Felicity was posting with perfect, easy rhythm. But she seemed to be making much motion compared to Ben's stillness.

"Ben has an uncanny sense of how it would be to be a horse," my father answered.

When Ben and Felicity rejoined us, my father gave me a leg up to my horse. "Now, one, two, jump!" he ordered, holding my left bent foreleg. With his boost and the spring I made off my right foot, I shot up so violently that I almost fell over the other side of the horse.

"I guess I'm still groggy from that terrible fall," I said loud enough to be sure Ben heard, as I struggled to find my seat and stirrups.

My father laughed. "I think *your* hair is very pretty. When you don't have sand in it."

I rode ahead beside Ben, with my father and Felicity following. I was glad for the chance to describe what had happened in my own way. "It's just lucky I wasn't killed," I told Ben as my perilous steed trudged along, head bobbing in semi-sleep. "This dumb thing bucked and reared and nobody, not even a cowboy, could have stayed on."

"What did you think on the way down?" Ben asked excitedly. "When you knew you were going to hit the ground?"

"I thought, 'how would it be to be a horse?'"

"What? Weren't you scared?"

"Of course—in a way. I knew I might be dead in a second. But, Ben, you never know what can come into your mind when you're facing death until it happens to you."

Ben looked back at my father. "It couldn't have been as bad as all that. He doesn't seem upset."

"I don't understand him at all," I said bitterly.

"Why? Because he isn't carrying on like Aunt Catherine after you 'faced death'?"

"No, it's not *just* that, Ben. It's just that...well..."

"What?! Honestly, Lucresse, you're the most irritating person I've ever met. *What* don't you understand?"

A quaking alarmed feeling went through me. I hadn't really meant to discuss explicitly what was bothering me. I wasn't sure there were words to explain the number of confusing images popping into my mind.

The nighttime Felicity was as enervated as the afternoon one was energetic. She was listless, sorrowful—sometimes, as much so as the first night we'd spent together—almost maudlin. She and my father never went out. Night after night, week after week, we spent séance-like interludes lying around the living room. When Ben and I went up to bed, Felicity always seemed more tired than we. Not much later—I lay awake listening for them—they would come up the steps, slowly, sleepily, not trying to smother their footsteps. Rarely were they talking. Not for fear of disturbing Ben and me, but seemingly because the act of retiring hardly disturbed the reverie we'd left them in. As I fell asleep, after I heard their doors close, I dwelt on the easy access they shared through the bathroom between their rooms. I wondered at the pattern her gold hair would make falling across his white-thatched head on the whiter pillowcase.

And now he'd said he thought her hair was hideous.

For several years I'd had a transcendent interest in sex relations. Other girls' interests were mild—giggling, social. So far as I knew, Fred's interest was nonexistent, and my father's was severely limited—to great loves in literature, humorous aspects of sexual desire, as revealed in reminiscences he and his friends found unfathomably funny, or, to unstimulating clinical explanations during the rare times when the subject came up. When we were much younger, Ben and I had speculated repeatedly about what men and women do, or might do. But not at all in the recent past. Nevertheless, Ben's interest was intact, I knew, and maybe even almost as profound as my own. He looked at, and over, girls, especially well-developed ones, with open pleasure. They, in turn, didn't seem to notice or find it important, as I did, that his ribcage extended only an eighth as far as his face indicated he imagined it had grown, and that his neck and legs were scrawny.

There on the horse, it occurred to me that the more Ben had learned about sexual activity, the less he talked about it with me.

"I don't understand why Daddy doesn't think Felicity is beautiful..." I said. My unspoken thought—if he wants to make love to her—still stuck in my throat.

Ben stiffened and swiveled in his saddle. "How do *you* know he doesn't think she's beautiful?"

"He told me so. I asked him."

Ben seemed appalled and unaccountably wounded. "What *right* did you have to ask him a thing like that?" he almost yelled. "He probably lied to you."

"I don't think so. He said she was a 'contrived work,' whatever that means. But he meant she isn't beautiful, and he said that her hair is 'hideous.' That's exactly what he said, Ben."

"He doesn't appreciate her," Ben said belligerently. "But a kid like you has no right to know that. *I've* known it from the beginning."

We rode for a few more paces. "Do *you* think she's beautiful, Ben?"

"Felicity is the most beautiful, wonderful woman in the world," pronounced Ben. "Lucresse, do you have any money?"

In addition to his other duties, Fred was keeper of the funds in our household. Wherever we lived, on the first day of residency, my father opened a bank account in the local bank, and Fred visited it every Monday morning to withdraw cash for the week. Fred kept it cached in a bilious-green tin box on a shelf in the closet in his room and doled it out to my father, Ben, and me, as requested. My father's requests were meager; he spent more than we did, but he charged everything. He needed cash only for tips and occasional periodicals. My requests were spasmodic, depending on passing whims and the time of the month. Ben's were the most frequent and depleting. He always had something to buy, in addition to the usual school lunches and notebook paper.

Fred's early youth supplied him with visions of a life endured in dark mines consequent to too-free spending, and he chafed at what he considered Ben's extravagance. Ben stopped asking him directly for funds and instead approached my father, who wasn't overly concerned about the extent or reasons. But my father had to ask Fred. It got so that, in return, Fred would ask if my father wanted the money for himself or for Ben.

It was at that junction, only a few months before we moved to Palm Beach, that, at Fred's suggestion, allowances were instituted for us. Though Ben's was four dollars, twice the amount of mine, I always had more on hand than he. I was always lending him money. And while we habitually bet a thousand or ten thousand or a million dollars on any subject of dispute, and the debts engaged in were never paid or meant to be paid, I felt serious about the dollar forty-five or eighty cents he owed me week to week. My father said I took after Fred.

But now, Ben's appeal for a loan was more sudden and urgent than usual. I knew books or an upcoming movie were not involved.

"Why do you want it?" I demanded.

"You wouldn't understand," he said. "How much do you have?

"Seven dollars and twenty cents."

"That might do it. I've got three. Are you going to let me have it or not?"

"All of it? What do you want it for, Ben?"

"If you must know, I've got to talk to Felicity, alone. I'm going to take her to lunch tomorrow."

"During lunch period?"

"I won't go back for the afternoon. This is more important than school. I may never go back."

"Ben!"

"I know you're too young to understand this, Lucresse, but can you keep a secret, for a little while anyway? Until tomorrow night?"

"I swear, Ben."

"I'm in love with Felicity. Insanely. Forever. And I know she's in love with me. The only thing that's been keeping us apart is Dad. I thought he was in love with her too. And I'm sure she thought so. Now are you going to give me the seven twenty or not?"

I stared at him.

"I told you you wouldn't understand," he said. "You're too immature. Well, are you going to give me the money and keep quiet, or not? You swore."

"I'll give it to you, but you've got to pay it back." I was overcome by the idea of a fifteen-year-old boy escaping from the school cafeteria to keep a rendezvous with a thirty-eight-year-old woman—a rendezvous meant to be never-ending. Ben's jaws were set with determination. His legs never looked so sticklike.

Except for "Good girl" when I gave him the money at home later, Ben said no more to me. During the evening, and in the morning, Felicity's behavior toward us all was no different than usual, and I was afire with curiosity and undirected pity. I didn't know whether I should feel sorry for my father because Felicity didn't love him, even though he didn't love her, or have a womanly compassion for her because she was to be informed that he didn't care for her as she'd thought he did, even though she didn't love *him*. I decided to focus my sympathy on my father. Whether he loved Felicity or not, whether he thought her hair hideous or not, he'd welcomed her as a warm companion of sorts. And wouldn't it surprise and humiliate him to discover that she wasn't satisfied to be of that value? And worse, that she'd found fuller fulfillment in his son?

The only one I didn't feel sorrow for was Ben. He was to be triumphant in the triumvirate. As always—I remembered his soloing in *Flowers of Spring*—he'd get what he wanted. I marveled at him. On the way to school the next morning, if he'd said he was going to make snow fall from the bright Florida sky, I would have believed he could. All I dared ask was, "*Is* Felicity going to meet you for lunch? Did you ask her?"

"Of course," he said. His thoughts seemed far away.

After a moment, I tried some more. "Ben, suppose your teacher asks me where you are? What should I say?"

"Say you don't know. You *won't* know."

"But, Ben—"

"Don't worry about it, Lucresse. I'm going to have to make a lot of arrangements. I'll check out of school myself, my own way. I *told* you, I have to speak to Felicity. And that's *all* I'm going to tell you."

"When are you going to tell Daddy?"

"As soon as possible, if Felicity agrees. Just remember, it's not up to you to tell him anything."

"When you've arranged everything, will you tell *me*?" I said anxiously.

"You'll hear about it."

Later that day at lunch period, I scanned the cafeteria for Ben. He wasn't there. I didn't even look for him after school. Instead I ran all the way home, expecting to find him already halfway through a heated, crucial three-way discussion of the future with my father and Felicity. She'd be holding Ben's hand. My father would be unable to look at them. The lines in his face would be deeper. Fred, having overheard everything, would be muttering to himself in the kitchen.

When I burst in, Fred was not there. Neither was Ben. My father and Felicity were in the living room. More accurately, he was in the living room, in his chair, very still, eyes cast down as I'd imagined, and Felicity was barging back and forth across the room, into the dining room, circling the table, and back into the living room, as though borne by a tornado, hair and hands flying, talking at the top of her voice.

"But where *is* he, Walter? Don't you understand that the boy is tortured! He *knows* I'm telling you about it! Who the hell knows what he's doing! And you *sit* there! *Hello,* Lucresse!"

"Where's Ben?" I asked.

"He'll come back," said my father.

"My God, Walter. I wish I was as sure as you. Haven't you ever been a *boy!?*"

"Not like Ben. I was a baby until I was forty."

I didn't think it possible for Felicity's voice to get louder, but it did. "This is no time for jokes, Walter! That poor kid might do anything. You should of seen him when he left me."

As innocently as I could, I inquired about what had happened—lighting the fuse to the extra store of dynamite in Felicity's heart.

"He *told* me he had to talk to me, alone!" she exploded. "Naturally I thought it was about some crazy thing about acting or something. He wanted to make it an event, so I said, 'Sure, Ben, I'll meet you for lunch,' and I wasn't s'posed to say anything about it so I didn't. How was I s'posed to know what was on his mind? The poor kid thinks he's in *love* with me! *That's* what's happening!"

She had referred to Ben as a "poor kid" twice too many times for me to now admit that I knew about their rendezvous. But I couldn't have interrupted her if I'd wanted to.

"He thought I was in love with him, only I didn't know it yet, he said. He wanted me to go away with him! We'd be happy together the rest of our lives—"

"Touring in *Candida* no doubt," my father interjected.

"I'm some type to play *Candida*!" bellowed Felicity. "Walter! Maybe *that's* it! Has he been reading *Candida*?"

"I don't know. But it's not convincing enough to trigger this," he said.

"Where is he?" I asked.

"We don't know," moaned Felicity. "I tried to set him right, but I guess I can't set anybody right. He ran out of the restaurant at ten of one and he didn't go back to school. I checked. Fred's out looking for him now."

"He'll find him," my father said. "He can't have gone far. He didn't have much money."

An unpleasant throbbing spasm seized my heart. "He borrowed seven dollars and twenty cents from me yesterday," I confessed. "And he already had three of his own."

"Then he had ten dollars and twenty cents," said my father. "That couldn't get him any further than Titusville, by bus, with eating."

"Did he pay for lunch, Felicity?" I asked.

"No. And he didn't eat his. That's another thing—Ben needs to put on weight. *Nothing* bothers you, Walter. Ben is too *thin*!"

"But Ben wouldn't want to go to Titusville," continued my father as though no one had spoken. "Even transported by desire, he wouldn't head for Titusville."

"Oh where *would* he go?" moaned Felicity. "The sweet little damn fool. I should've told him he and me were meant for each other and brought him back home! Lucresse, stop standing there."

I was confused.

"Put down your books!" she bellowed.

I carried my books to the laden table behind the sofa and moved the day's mail to make room for them. The mail hadn't been opened, and one letter caught my eye. The familiar deliberate penmanship and address: "Mr. Walter Briard & Family." It was Aunt Catherine's monthly communication. I opened it and read it to the accompaniment of Felicity and my father talking, but not to each other—just thinking aloud in each other's presence. From the violet stationery, I could hear Aunt Catherine's voice punctuating their soliloquies with irrelevant remarks:

—Joe has had a terrible cold ever since the last week in September. And I've been thinking of you all in sunny Florida. That's a good place

to be for anybody that's given to taking colds and I hope you've all found it real happy there...

"Where would he *go*?" wailed Felicity. "A kid like that, after a knock like that?"

...Joe and I have hardly gone out anywhere, what with his cold, sneezing and coughing and getting him up in the nights, except to Tulsa for the Legion dinner last Saturday night, and we had to go to that 'cause Flo Daggett was chairman of food. I told you about her last month. She's the one that thinks she makes the best potato pancakes in the whole world?...

I didn't recall Daggett or pancakes, but Aunt Catherine's letters always abounded with references to local personalities who were strangers to us.

"Ben watches Ben," my father declared. "He isn't foolish. Whatever he does, he does well. He'll take disappointment well."

...Anyways, Joe thinks what with how things have been, and me doing all the work getting Flo to let Lucy Cummings make the potato pancakes, who really makes them so much better and keeping old Mrs. Dunhamly out of the way—of course it's time I got out of this dreary winter weather for a spell...

"You go *mashugana* the first time you think you're in love," Felicity said. "With me, it was Leon Rosenblatt. He was a great big healthy, shy boy. He played basketball and was going to night school to be an accountant. I used to daydream that he loved me and his name was different and he played polo, and I told my mother I wouldn't spit on him."

...So he's been after and after me, till finally he made me see my way clear to taking out for a visit with all of you in the near future. Let's hope all goes well—with the drugstore I mean, and Joe's cold—and I'll plan on being there on December the eight...

"It won't take him long to stop hating us," my father said. "The real problem is to figure out where he'd go to work on it."

"Walter, why don't we call up some of his friends or that dramatics teacher of his?" Felicity begged.

...It always does my heart good to think of seeing poor Jen's loved ones. Did I tell you they're thinking of building a new airport here? Right across from the cemetery? Well, did Joe and me put up an argument! Some people just have no respect for the dead...

"More likely he'd be talking to strangers right now," my father said.

"If he was *my* boy," Felicity ranted, "I wouldn't leave him to talk his heart out to strangers. I wouldn't let him meet up with a woman like me for his first crush."

...so it's still up in the air what they're going to do. I did want to tell you all though, Jen's grave is the prettiest one there, and the little holly hedge around it is green as can be even in the bad weather we've been having...

A car in the driveway arrested all voices. Car door slammed. Front door banged open. It was Fred. Alone. No one—at the bus terminal, railroad station, airlines, or at three classmates' houses—had seen Ben.

Fred was close to frantic. "Mr. Briard, it is five o'clock," he said, trembling. "I do hope the lad hasn't gone strolling near the docks. There is just no telling what villain he may have encountered—" Fred's antipathy to sun and sea extended to the entire segment of mankind with anything to do with either. Such people—dock workers, fishermen, boatmen, and their near-laced relatives—had potentialities of evil unguessed by more civilized folk.

"You have a very good point there!" My father perked up—surprisingly, because for years, he had been disputing Fred's opinion of sea-faring people, always insisting that they were no better or worse than anybody else.

Fred's next thought was too terrible to speak aloud. "You don't think he's been *shanghaied*?" he whispered.

"No," said my father emphatically.

"Then what, for God's sake?" Felicity shouted, loud enough to hurt my head.

Unhearing due to the drama in *his* head, Fred blinked and elaborated. "Bound head and hand to foot in the bottom of a boat," he lamented.

"Oy gevalt!" Felicity moaned. "What're you gonna do, Walter? Wait till it's too late? Call the *cops!*"

"Use your head, Felicity!" My father pointed at her angrily. "It's possible to figure out *some* things in life by *thinking!*" He pounded his own head with the finger he'd used to scorn hers. "Ben's not on the way to Cuba!"

"How the hell do *you* know?!" she blazed back at him.

"Call it an educated guess!" he bellowed over his shoulder. "If Fred and I aren't back by dinnertime, you two eat!" And he and Fred were out the door.

After the sound of the car faded, Felicity was odd—distraught, but quietly so. For the love of Ben, the walls had resounded with screaming, and now, for the same reason, I could hear the rustling of the palms outside and the low hum of the icebox three rooms away.

Felicity sat stone-still, dark eyes blank with misery, hands fallen in her lap, ostensibly unaware that she wasn't alone. All for the love of Ben. I told myself that she needed my comfort.

But what I said was far more truthful. "Don't worry like that, Felicity. Ben's all right. I'm sure he is. He's *always* all right. *Ben* never gets in trouble he can't get out of."

Very slowly, her lids lifted until her eyes were looking into mine. It was as though her eyes could see through mine into an area inside that was mysterious even to me.

"Don't worry so much about *yourself*, Lucresse," she said. "He may have hurt your feelings now and then—"

"Now and *then*?" I exploded, the mysterious area suddenly exposed in a flood of light. I was so angry I could taste it—at Ben for being the focus of her and everyone's attention and, even more confusing, at Felicity...for what?

"...but he loves you," continued Felicity. "And now *his* feelings have been hurt."

I tried to switch the light off fast. "And Daddy's hurt *your* feelings. That's what I really meant. He had no right to be so mean to you."

"He wasn't being mean, Lucresse. He was making me feel better. Trying to believe *himself* that there are no consequences, serious consequences, for what I did."

"But, Felicity, you didn't *do* anything," I said, truly believing it and completely forgetting my feelings of two seconds before.

"I moved in here, didn't I? So it was fine for me to have you all help me get rid of Mead, wasn't it? But did I think how it was for a little boy that didn't know his mother? A boy all spiffed up ready and dying for a woman?"

"But Ben and *you*..." I said, unable to fit the combination into any context.

"If anything has happened to Ben..." she said, drifting off, her eyes dull and despairing again.

"Nothing has," I insisted, all at once hoping that nothing had—and suddenly it didn't matter that Ben was the apex of everyone's attention.

It was six o'clock. Sometime after that, I asked Felicity if she'd let me help her fry a chicken that was quartered and ready in the icebox. She said no, and I ate a banana and two bowls of chocolate pudding. She wouldn't eat a thing. She smoked about fourteen cigarettes and wouldn't even answer when I asked if she wanted a drink.

It was past seven the next time I looked at the clock, and all I know is that, from then on, life turned into a tornado of sound and motion that had no counterpart in my experience. Peak emotion, no holds barred, no inhibitions respected, no word or action withheld. Doors slammed—the car was in the front—feet scuffled, dragged, and kicked as Fred and my father lugged a roaring drunk, flailing Ben into the house. Bodies jammed and banged and dropped as they lifted and pushed and shoved him up the staircase, knocking into each other, with Felicity and me following cautiously behind. Ben's hair hung wet over his streaming eyes, his shirt was open and torn. And the whole time, at the top of his lungs, he sang, "Laugh, Clown, Laugh," and screamed, "Let me go!" while punching the closest body or wall or air with loose, aimless fists.

My father yelled. So did Fred.

"Oh, Ben! Oh, Ben!" wept Felicity at each step, and with her own fists, threatened the Fates in Yiddish for Ben's inebriated state. Then, in a mixture of Yiddish and English, she raged at my father for taking so long, but thanked God and him for finding Ben.

My father boomed directions to Fred, swatted back at Ben, and yelled a disjointed explanation to Felicity and me about how and where they'd recovered Ben.

Struggling with his part of the writhing load, Fred dodged Ben's and my father's blows and prattled comforting understatements in a shrill singsong: "Only two more little steps, my boy... There now, you're not so bad off, are you? ...Only two more little, now... Here we go, see? You're already looking better. Just a dash of a tub and you'll be fit as a fiddle...whatho?... Now, one more little step; righto, my boy?..."

Finally, they got Ben into the bathroom between his and my room and lowered him into the tub. Fred held him down while my father turned on the shower. Ben bubbled and sputtered and screamed, "Gi'me liberty or gi' me death!" and finally quieted. Fred remained holding him, making soothing noises, the same ones he'd made when we'd suffered the falls and bruises of early childhood. And my father and Felicity and I adjourned to Ben's bedroom.

"My God, Walter, how much do you think he's had?" said Felicity, unwilling to risk a guess.

"In the shack called the Dock-Rest, where he was, ten dollars and twenty cents could have bought him seventeen. But the captain—the barman who owns the place—told me he bought two rounds for the regular crew that hang around all the time. They number four or five, so Ben probably hasn't put down more than nine or ten himself."

"Ten!" exclaimed Felicity. "I'm an old hand and five leave me shaking."

"You know," my father said, "Ben has real stick-to-it-iveness. He became quite sick around four o'clock, but he came right back for more, the captain told me. He's a good man—in spite of what Fred thinks. He was prepared to put Ben up for the night."

There was a moan, a splash. Fred opened the door and Ben's voice, muffled and mixed with running water and Fred's running chatter, came clearly: "I'm cold...it's cold in here...I'm shivering. If Dad had one ounce of warmth in his heart, I wouldn't be freezing this way! Oh, Felicity...Felicity! You don't know how I'm freezing. "

Disheveled but triumphant, Fred joined us in Ben's bedroom. "He's sobered now," he informed us. "But he insists on getting into his robe himself." Then, shaking his head, Fred headed downstairs, pulling his soaked shirt away from his body like a particularly vile second skin.

"*I* can talk to him," Felicity said, pushing my father and me out into the hall. She left the door open at a seventy-degree angle, and, by leaning slightly to the left, we saw her burst into the steamy bathroom and embrace Ben with iron arms.

"Oh, Ben...Ben...my little Ben," she crooned. "Someday you'll find a nice girl, someday, God willing."

Ben began to cry. "I don't want a *nice* girl," he sobbed into her shoulder.

Stroking his tear-sodden cheeks, Felicity led him into his room and to his bed. She sat at his side, still touching his face with her palm. "You'll be so happy," she said. "With a *young* girl, who'll learn everything *with* you—"

"I don't want a *young* girl," said Ben sleepily.

"A girl that's just *right*, a girl like Lucresse," crooned Felicity.

Ben right-angled up to a sitting position, his face stricken dry. "Like Lucresse?!" Then he thrust himself face-first into the pillow and moaned inconsolably.

Felicity caressed the back of his head, slowly, thoughtfully, and finally came out to us, closing the door silently behind her. "He'll be all right when he wakes up. I think he understood what I said."

"Maybe," my father said. "It's time we all went to bed."

My father and Felicity went to their rooms, silently, through the separate doors. And I went to mine.

I was glad Ben was back. I was glad Felicity felt better about what she thought she had done. I was glad my father wasn't unduly upset about what had happened, that he'd swatted Ben back when Ben had punched him on the staircase, that he admired Ben as always, this time for his "stick-to-it-iveness." The only circumstance I was not glad about was what Felicity had said, and what Ben now believed: that someday he'd find a girl like me.

Sitting in my own bed, listening to Ben's pillow-stifled cries through our adjoining bathroom, I almost cried for him. Finally, unable to stand it, I got out of bed, crept through our two bathroom doors into his room. Ben's face was hidden in the pillow, but he turned it toward the wall as I tiptoed over to him.

"Wha'd'*you* want?" he mumbled.

"Are you awake, Ben?"

"Christ, no."

"I wanted you to know I know how you feel."

"Swell."

"And what Felicity said will happen. It won't."

"You had no right to listen to what she said."

"I couldn't help it."

He sighed deeply.

"Ben?"

"Yes?"

"You'll find a nicer girl than me. There are a lot of them."

He turned over, as though his sharp bones weighed a thousand pounds. He squinted at me and wiped a hand across his eyes. "No. There aren't many," he said finally and smiled.

My throat hurt too much to talk, so I just smiled too. He closed his eyes again.

"The only trouble with Felicity is that she has no imagination," he said sleepily. "That's why she was such a flop as an actress."

"She would have been a nice mother though," I said.

"That's right. *You* have more imagination than she has." He breathed long and decisively. "If I don't go to sleep, I'm going to be sick again."

I laid my hand on his head the way I'd seen Felicity do, then went back to my room, glowing with the heady knowledge that somehow I'd acquired the splendid asset of imagination. I lay in bed marveling at it and restored by the thought that all was well again, as it had been before the devil—romance—attacked Ben. And I forgot entirely about Aunt Catherine's letter until just before I, too, fell asleep.

CHAPTER FIVE: AN ENDING

A miserable sobriety descended on Ben and Felicity the next day. It even touched my father and Fred. All were subdued and withdrawn. No one referred to the explosive events of the night before. I thought any change that could be brought about—through a new thought, new news—was bound to alter the mood for the happier, and the only news I could think of was Aunt Catherine's letter.

Perhaps it was because of the time of day—midafternoon, Felicity's high point of every twenty-four hours—that the news of Aunt Catherine's visit was accepted as good and cheering. It was ten minutes before my father mentioned, as though it was of the utmost unimportance, "Of course she'll have to share your room, Lucresse."

"And how do we explain *me*?" said Felicity, delving deeper into the subject. "How do we explain me in the guest room?"

"You have a job here," quipped my father.

"What kind of job?" Ben said, looking threatening.

Ignoring him, my father addressed Felicity alone. "You've said you thought my accounts are in sad need of a neatening hand."

"And they are."

"All right then," my father declared as though it were settled. "That's something Catherine will surely understand. You are my accountant, secretarial assistant, or clean-up squad if you prefer."

"Clean-up squad will do," Felicity said.

Over the ensuing weeks, Felicity became absorbed by her new calling. She unwrinkled vintage bills and orders and receipts. She recovered more recent forms recording payment for pieces of merchandise my father had sold, swift notations on the last time Ben and I had seen a dentist, and a two-paragraph command for cremation, ostensibly an "important document" of my father's (which he'd assumed he'd lost) to be enacted in the eventuality of his demise. All of these and several hundred other papers that defied categorizing, Felicity, in silk, apricot-colored beach pajamas, was putting into perfectly constructed pyramids on the study floor on December eighth when Aunt Catherine arrived.

Aunt Catherine's meeting with Felicity inspired Ben to hurry off early to school, to wheedle his speech teacher into letting him play a dual role in a forthcoming school production which would usurp all of his afternoon hours. But my father stood his ground. For a while during the first moments of the Aunt Catherine/Felicity introduction, I thought he might actually spend more time on the scene than was his custom when Aunt Catherine was on our premises—her reaction to his live-in "assistant" was so striking.

Lingering at breakfast with Felicity, my father, and me, Aunt Catherine instructed us all on the comparative disadvantages of being seated up front, in the middle, and at the back of a cross-country bus: back was bumpiest, middle was already taken, in front one had to abide the driver's abuse of laymen drivers. My father cut in saying, "No more, Catherine. Never more. Finally, by your own admission, you *must* try air travel. I'm going to make you. I'll get the ticket for your return."

"Yes, Walter, yes," she replied, preoccupied with inspecting Felicity across the table. Felicity smiled at her and went on eating her toast.

"Have you been doing this kind of—uh—sec'etarial work long, Miss Peddicord?" Aunt Catherine asked.

"*Mrs.* Peddicord," Felicity said, chewing. "No, I haven't, though it's the kind of work I looked for for years."

"Oh?"

"Yes," Felicity said. "I always yearned to be of assistance to someone."

"Oh?"

"I just never knew where my talent lay before I met the Briards."

My father, aiming at Felicity's ankle under the table, kicked mine by accident.

Aunt Catherine gave a short, shrill giggle. "I certainly do see where it'd take a lot of talent to sort out all *his* stuff," she complimented.

"Of course that's not *all* I do, to assist." Felicity raised her large eyelids very slowly and directed a limpid stare into Aunt Catherine's inquisitive face. "I play sort of nursemaid too."

Here, Aunt Catherine felt on more solid ground. "Really?" she said. "Y'know, at home, most of the folks that keep nursemaids, the young oil folks, they try to get English-type girls, like Fred is. You hardly ever do see a Latin kind of type like you, Mrs. Peddicord."

"Latin?" A battering laugh burst out of Felicity. "So you noticed the hair job? I've only had one touch-up since I've been here. But, Mrs. Tippet, I'm a far cry from Latin. Try again."

My father kicked me again, and this time I let him know it with a pleading ouch.

"I beg your pardon?" Aunt Catherine said politely.

"I'm Jewish. It's one of the faiths. Real old one. Predates vaudeville."

"Oh, yes—of course, I *know*," Aunt Catherine said. "We have many people of the Jewish faith in Oklahoma."

"In cages?"

"My goodness, no. Indeed, no," Aunt Catherine replied quickly. "They're all very fine people."

"No one's a louse?" asked Felicity, incredulous.

By the time I left for school, my father was making telephone calls and plans to drive to Boynton Beach for the day. And that night, from the twin bed next to mine, Aunt Catherine whispered, "Don't trust that Peddicord woman, Lucresse. She's not what she's making out to be. I can tell. No Jew-woman wants to be a sec'etary-nursemaid."

During the next week, there was a noticeable depletion of our household goods. My father made selling appointments by the dozen. He and Fred were gone a good part of every day, and two sets of china that always moved with us disappeared. Also a pair of Chinese ivory back-scratchers, the silver napkin rings that had originated in Louis XIV's silversmith's shop and had last been used as building and balancing toys by Ben and me, and a Renaissance multicolored vase left the house.

"Just see that you don't find a customer for that Greek's cowbell," Felicity said one night. "I'm taking that with me when I leave."

It was then that I knew that Felicity would not be with us forever.

Not forty-eight hours later she told me, alone, on the upstairs landing—she was going the next morning, early, by taxi, and I was not to get up to say good-bye. "I've caused enough trouble here," she said. "I've already told Ben."

CHAPTER SIX: ROBBERY

I meant to mind her. But Aunt Catherine clattered across my room to the window before the morning light had reached my bed. And then I heard the bonging.

When I got both eyes open, Aunt Catherine was peeking through my pale white curtains and her back looked alarmed. I scurried out of bed and joined her.

"I'm sorry I woke you up," she whispered. "But I couldn't see the whole path from my window. Will you just look at that!"

A car was parked on our driveway and Felicity and my father were walking on the path toward it, slowly, dallying as they went. He had on slippers, pajamas, and his old silk bathrobe, and was carrying her suitcase. She was wearing a bright yellow dress and carrying the heavy iron and bronze Athenian cowbell she had so admired. With each step, it tolled a low reverberating bong, which seemed to amuse both of them.

"I knew there was something about that woman," Aunt Catherine whispered. "Taking the bell with her. She's a common thief, that's what she is."

"He must have *given* it to her, Aunt Catherine," I said.

"Sure! She talked him out of it. I swear that man'd let any thief and robber on earth talk him out of anything right in front of his nose."

My father kissed Felicity on the cheek and put her suitcase in the car. She got in, with a final, louder bong, and they both laughed again, on either side of the closed door, as the car pulled away.

"I knew that was no kind of housekeeper-woman. She was nothing but a fancy robber."

It was impossible to convince her otherwise without telling her the truth about Felicity's visit, so I remained silent. But years later, I often wondered if Aunt Catherine assumed Felicity had something to do with the subsequent armed invasion.

It was just a few nights after Felicity's departure. Ben and I were on the scene because, one, while my father had always included us in his adult company, he genuinely welcomed our participation during Aunt Catherine's stays—possibly because our chatter permitted him to remain quiet without being impolite. And two, because Fred, who'd always seen to it that we went to bed at some fairly reasonable time, had recently begun to retire early. A doctor he'd consulted about a wax deposit in one ear had pried out not only the wax but Fred's admission that he was fatigued lately. To justify his bill, the M.D. had prescribed more rest and a bottle of pills to encourage it. So now Fred, having uncritically endured decades of my father's erratic schedule, hurried with righteous enjoyment to his isolated room off the kitchen and into deep, undisturbable sleep as soon as he finished the dinner dishes and admonished Ben and me, "Half past nine o'clock. Precisely. Remember now."

Aunt Catherine was vigilantly mindful of this order, consulting the English ding-clock on the mantel every little while and calling out the extent of our remaining freedom. This evening, as our parole elapsed, we worked hard to invigorate the conversation. When Aunt Catherine sang, "Five minutes, children," (we ignored her insult to our respective fourteen and fifteen years, knowing that her habits of speech were intractable) and talk was again lagging, I got desperate.

"Know what happened to me today?" I said brightly, drawing on an experience I might otherwise have kept to myself.

"What?" said Aunt Catherine, glancing once more at the clock.

"I swallowed a flea."

"A flea!" she gasped.

"A *live* one?" asked Ben. He was being helpful, but also, someday he could be called upon to demonstrate how a person who swallowed a flea behaves, and he used every opportunity to prepare for his impending career as a famous actor.

"I'm not sure," I said. "It was on the way home from the beach. The wind was blowing and I couldn't tell whether it was *blowing* him or he was *flying*. But all of a sudden, he swooped right into my mouth. And before I could think to spit him out, I swallowed."

"Good heavens!" said Aunt Catherine.

"But do you *guess* he was alive?" Ben persisted.

"I don't *know*. I *just said*, 'before I could *think*.'"

"Why was your mouth open and your mind closed?" asked my father.

"I guess I was just breathing," I said, fearing that the subject may have run its course.

Ben didn't let it. "Do you *have* your mouth open and your brain turned off when you breathe?"

"I don't usually think about breathing when I do it," I argued back happily.

"For heaven's sake!" Aunt Catherine shuddered retroactively.

Ben struck a dramatic, contemplative pose. "Actually, there isn't anything very world-shaking about swallowing a flea," he declared with the full authority of a professor. "Even a live one. When you think of the number of microorganisms all of us must swallow every day. The classified germs alone probably run into the thousands. And when you consider the *un*classified ones..."

"Lord have mercy," Aunt Catherine murmured.

"That'll be enough, Ben," my father said.

And that's when the door buzzer sounded. For a second we weren't certain it had sounded. It was the barely tapped timid note struck by a stranger who isn't sure he has the right house or that he isn't awakening sleeping occupants. My father ambled to answer it, and at once, we saw that it wasn't a stranger but was two—both quite young, quite nervous—men, one a head taller than the other. The taller one carried a large, cardboard-packing carton, and the shorter one held a dull, metal pistol in his right hand, pointed straight at my father's wide chest.

Without a word, they all moved into the living room, the young men advancing, my father backing up. Maybe it was the shock, but the robbers struck me as ludicrous—like puppet mice forcing an oversized puppet lion, my father, to retreat in some kind of make-believe puppet show. It was so silly I might have giggled if Ben hadn't suddenly dropped his professor pose and stopped acting, and Aunt Catherine's face hadn't gone whiter than the curtains in our shared bedroom.

As if by unspoken agreement that we too were puppets in this show, Ben and I simultaneously stood.

"Everybody go over to that side of the room and nobody gets hurt," the short one said.

In one perfectly choreographed move, my father backed up all the way to the mantel and Ben and I joined him, nobody taking their eyes off the robbers.

"I said *everybody*!" barked the short one, bobbing the gun at Aunt Catherine who seemed to be glued to her chair. With a jump, she came unstuck and ran on bird-toes to my side, where she reglued herself to my shoulder.

The taller robber wandered casually around the room, swinging his carton. "C'mon. Let's get going," he said to his partner.

"Okay," the short one replied. He kept his stance facing us, the gun aimed at my father, but his eyes scanned the room, lighting on a huge, rectangular, seventeenth-century French tapestry on the one unornamented wall. "Get that," he ordered the tall one.

Like a monkey after a banana, the tall one scaled the bookcase to reach the tapestry's hooks. He released them, and he and the tapestry dropped with two thuds to the floor. Then grabbing two corners of the heavy cloth, he started to fold.

"You don't fold that," said my father, loudly, agreeably, only slightly wavering. "You roll it, son."

The monkey-man froze, squinted at my father, then looked to his partner.

"Do like he says," said the short one. "You gotta treat this stuff right."

"Why does that tapestry always have to be rolled?" Ben asked my father, in the curious, conversational way he might have asked such a question at any time.

"Because those threads have been stretched for more than three hundred years. They're liable to break if they're bent sharply," my father replied, the waver gone.

The monkey-man spread the cloth on the floor and fell to all fours, rolling it. "C'mon, what else?" he said, breathing heavily. "This could take all night."

Our short, armed supervisor looked far right and left. "That over there in the corner," he ordered. "Get that." He gestured with his eyes at an enormous, tarnished serving tray that Fred customarily grumblingly stored on the floor since no pantry cabinet was large enough to house it, and no shelf was strong enough to support its weight. For years, he'd been after my father to sell it.

My father shook his head. "Frankly, I think it would be ill-advised to take that," he said reasonably.

Our shorter visitor braced his thick legs further apart and lifted his aiming hand an inch. "Why?" he demanded.

"Because, son, you'd have a very difficult time carting it in that carton." My father spoke patiently, almost kindly. "And an even more difficult time selling it."

"Oh, I don't know," the short one said suspiciously. "We got a guy—"

"I know. Of course, it's up to you, but I can tell you a little about it. That's an authentic Cellini, all right..." He hesitated, thoughtful. "Real silver, that is. But nobody wants to buy it. I've tried to sell it all over the world."

"So, if it's real authentic silver," said the squat young man with the pistol, "why don't nobody want to buy it?"

"Because it's probably the one downright hideous Cellini piece in existence." My father spoke confidently. "If you look at it, really look at it, you'll see that it could have been made by any third-rate, sixteenth-century silversmith."

The young man with the gun glanced at the tray again, now in the straining arms of his associate. "Yeah. It *is* ugly. Okay. Put it down, Frank."

"What?" Frank said, incredulous. "Hey, listen. We gotta get goin'!"

The short one waved the gun impatiently. "I *said* put it down."

Aunt Catherine clutched my arm in a death grip as she bit her lower lip and blinked hard to clear the fast-coming tears.

"Ow," I murmured as she dug her nails into my bone, and Frank banged the heavy tray to the floor.

"Jeez!" he grunted angrily. "And what's the idea callin' me Frank?!"

"Shut up and pack those," the short one said, indicating an assortment of silver forks, demitasse spoons, and carved-handled knives tied together with narrow silk ribbon and employed as a paperweight for the day's newspapers on the marble coffee table.

"You had no right to call me by my name, *Sled*-boy," Frank spat viciously.

"All right. So, you called me *my* name," Sled-boy said.

"But that's not a real name, like Frank."

"Everybody *calls* me Sled-boy, don't they?" the short one reasoned. "And *we* know *their* name's Briard, don't we?"

"May I present my son, Ben, my daughter, Lucresse, and my sister-in-law, Mrs. Tippet?" said my father, as though he were hosting a dinner party.

"How do you do?" I said.

"Oh, Walter," whimpered Aunt Catherine, sucking in a sob.

Ben stepped forward extending his hand. "Glad to meet you, Sled-boy, Frank."

With a hurried, embarrassed motion, Sled-boy transferred his gun to his left hand and gave Ben a fast handshake.

"For Chris' sake, are we doin' a job here or not?" said Frank.

"Say, you know what you *could* sell easily, and would be no trouble carrying in that carton?" Ben said to Sled-boy, as if collaborating with a best friend or a brother on a household chore.

"What?" said Sled-boy.

"Books!" said Ben brightly. "There are lots of *very* valuable books here. And we've been in stores where they'll buy *anything*."

"That's true," said my father helpfully, "but before you get in a rush about it, I think you ought to give books more careful consideration."

"How do you mean, Mr. Briard?" said Sled-boy, looking at my father with an expression I couldn't quite understand. Admiration? Fascination? Affection?

"Perhaps if we all sat down," suggested my father congenially, "we could analyze the problem properly." And he gestured for our visitors to make themselves comfortable.

"Walter! Really!" Aunt Catherine gasped.

Frank shot her a commiserating look. "Yeah, lady. You'd think this was a tea party or something."

In response, Aunt Catherine dug her bony fingers even deeper into my skinny arm. I wiggled with pain, and she gave me a withering look.

Sled-boy remained braced, thinking, contemplative—almost the way Ben had been when playing the professor before our visitors' surprising entrance. Then, deciding he might as well comply, he sat on the edge of the wing-chair near him and laid his gun in his lap. With a sigh, my father eased himself into his usual club chair and crossed his legs. To restore my circulation, I unclutched Aunt Catherine's fingers from my bicep and sat on the arm of my father's chair while she maintained her rigid stance by the wall. And Frank, almost recalcitrant, leaned against the woodwork of the doorway. Seeing his objecting attitude, Aunt Catherine clamped closed her eyes to shut out the sight of him and all else. Ben, afire with interest in the proceedings, scraped the desk chair over as close to Sled-boy as he could.

"Now," my father said, as we were all settled, "Ben's suggestion of books has merit. Provided one is aware of the needs and practices of the 'stores' he has in mind." He smiled at Ben, who seemed to glow with the compliment, and like a twin brother, Sled-boy seemed to follow suit, leaning in to hear my father's advice. "One practice of dealers in rare books is that they often take years to pay for their purchases," my father continued. "Which is understandable. It often takes them years to resell a book. Nevertheless, Ben, your idea shows straight and speedy thought."

As Ben glowed and Frank, still standing at the doorway, listened, his face became more boyish somehow, softer, eager—as though he too had the queer feeling that he was playing in some sort of a show, where he was like Ben, a brother boy puppet, whose father was saying something nice about him and to him.

I had a funny feeling in that place deep inside, that mysterious place behind my eyes where Felicity had once seen me. But I blinked several times and it soon disappeared.

"I must admit," my father said, returning Frank's soft and interested gaze, "I don't know much about your field of business, son. But yours and mine are both trades, of a sort."

"And you know *yours*, all right," Ben said, smiling broadly.

Frank relaxed against the doorpost as the dreaminess on his face invaded his body. His puppet-brother had said something nice to their father. I, too, felt persuaded that the admiration glowing between Ben and my father was extraordinary and usual with them, although I couldn't recall the last time they had exchanged such open, ready compliments.

"It seems to me that you fellows ought to limit your product to something that is, one, transportable; two, nonidentifiable; and, three, and above all, negotiable."

"I think you're right, Mr. Briard," Frank said loudly. "This job sure wasn't *my* idea. Sled-boy says there's a fortune here, and he's got the guy for it. But from the beginning, I says, I don' know."

"So's what would you limit the product to, Mr. Briard?" Sled-boy spoke up, with newly distinct diction.

My father sat far back in his chair, poked his thumbs through his belt, and smiled. "Only one product I know qualifies. Cash."

"Cash," Sled-boy repeated thoughtfully, as though receiving advice from his accountant. "Yeah, you don't need no big box to carry it, and you can spend it right away without waiting around on nobody. That's real good advice, Mr. Briard." He crossed his legs the same way my father's were crossed. "I don't yen to make a job more complicated than it has to be and maybe get sent up."

"You are a very sensible young man," my father said admiringly, and the uncomfortable feeling that I'd blinked away from behind my eyes moved down to my chest.

"Okay!" barked Frank, sounding almost jealous of Sled-boy. "So, it's smart to take cash. So, we take cash and forget about the other junk you were so hot on. Okay. So, let's get the cash. Where is it, Mr. Briard?"

My father looked pained. "That's the only trouble, here," he said. "I never keep cash on hand. Oh, I must have two or three dollars in my pocket. But that would hardly be worth your while."

"C'mon now," Frank said, "how can a man have a million dollars' worth of junk around and not have cash?"

"Dear heaven," Aunt Catherine muttered. Her shoulders were shaking.

"Because he doesn't *use* cash much," Ben said, giving Frank the disdainful look he frequently used on me. He turned to Sled-boy. "That's right. Nobody in our house, besides Lucresse, ever has any money because they charge everything. And all she's got is her allowance."

"You believe that?" Frank said to Sled-boy.

Sled-boy seemed to want to believe it, but sense was getting in the way of desire. He examined my father's face. My father smiled genially. He examined mine. I tried to imitate my father's expression, but it turned weak and stupid as the icky feeling in my chest moved down to my stomach, and I wondered if my father liked these two robbers better than me. What a silly feeling, I thought, but it remained lodged in my stomach like a stone.

Frank rose to his psychological advantage. "Okay, Sled-boy. You've run things so far. Now I take over. You keep them here, and I'll search the place. You can't tell *me* there's no cash in a layout like this." He started for the door to the den.

"Frank, I'll make a bet with you," Ben said.

Frank wheeled around. "What kind of bet?"

Ben turned to me enthusiastically. "How much do you have in your drawer?"

"I don't know," I said.

"You *always* know."

"About four dollars and sixty-five cents, I think."

"Okay. Frank, I'll bet you her four dollars and sixty-five cents that we don't have another nickel anywhere in this house, except what's in my father's pocket, and, here—" he pulled a crumpled dollar out of his pants—"what's in mine. If you *do* find more, it's yours. If you *don't*, you give us four dollars and sixty-five cents. Okay?"

"What we ought to do is call the police," said Aunt Catherine quietly.

"Y'see? *You* said this'd be easy," Frank said to Sled-boy.

Sled-boy dutifully leveled his gun at Aunt Catherine. She buried her head in her arms, trembling.

"Of course she isn't going to call anyone," my father said comfortingly. "Frank, do you accept Ben's bet or not?"

"Why not?" Sled-boy said.

"Sure," Frank said. "Dammit, if there's dough here, I'm gonna find it."

"That's the spirit!" Ben said.

"To be certain that the bet is perfectly fair, let's see how much I actually *do* have on my person." My father dug into his trousers' pocket, and extracted some wrinkled bills and a few coins, then drew the pocket and the one on the other side inside out. He put the bills and change in a basket-woven china dish on the lamp table next to his chair. "Exactly two dollars and seventeen cents."

"Okay," Frank said, and sprinted out of the room into the den.

I traced his search by the lights that went on throughout the house. But he hardly made a sound. I couldn't stop thinking that it was a pity Frank hadn't taken up ballet dancing—he was so lithe.

"Catherine, won't you please sit down?" my father said. "It may be quite a wait."

She perched on a corner of the sofa, grasping its arm with clawed fingers. Her cheeks looked like cement.

"Try to relax, Catherine," he said more kindly.

I could see by the light trail that Frank was in Ben's room, and I couldn't stay out of things any longer. "He won't find anything in there," I said, "except a bunch of plays and books on acting."

"And of course those are of no value whatever," said Ben, fuming.

"They're not money. You make fun of me for saving money, but you *never* have any."

"My son's going to be a very successful actor," my father explained to Sled-boy. "But I'm afraid he'd better find himself a very cautious business manager or he'll never accumulate any money. Or, then again, Ben, it's just possible that you may turn into the most penurious, penny-pinching actor yet known."

"An actor, huh?" Sled-boy mused. "I once knew a guy, was in all the plays in high school when I went. A real good lookin' guy. He was gonna get in the movies. You know what? His old man gave him two hundred bucks, for nothin' except to go out to California. An' you know what? The guy damn near starved to death. I think he finally got a job at Lockheed." Sled-boy raised and resettled his thick thighs, one at a time. "Mr. Briard, how come you're so sure your boy there gonna be such a big success? You know some big Hollywood producer or somebody?"

My father laughed. "No. If I did, I certainly would recommend Ben to him, when he's ready. Not that it would do him any good in the long run."

"I don't want anybody's help," Ben said.

"That's a very proper, immature attitude, and a very easy one to have when you don't need help, Ben. But Sled-boy asked me how I know you'll be successful. It's apparent."

"Why, Dad?"

I was as interested in the answer as I was in the question. I had known from the moment, years before, on some church steps in some now almost forgotten town, that Ben was going to be an actor. It had never occurred to me that he wouldn't be a successful actor. My reasoning being that there weren't actors who didn't appear any more than there were plumbers who didn't do plumbing.

"Success, as we categorize it, is a simple and pitiable thing," my father said. "It's only a matter of degree of wanting, and accident. Wanting plays the major role in everybody's life—accident all the others. The only condition any of us can be sure of in this universe is wanting. How tepid or burning hot the want is depends on accident.

But since accident isn't really as accidental as we'd like to think—accident is the great fooler and comforter of mankind—we become 'successful' exactly to the degree we want."

Sled-boy bent forward, concentrating. "But, Mr. Briard, say a guy like me wants, really wants, like hell, a lot of things. A house like this ...say he wants, well, to be a guy like you, when he's your age."

"One moment, Sled-boy. The first thing one must want, in order to gain anything, is to be *himself*, gaining. Don't confuse sterile wishing with true wanting. I think it was Dryden who described that mistake: 'I strongly wish for what I faintly hope: / Like the day-dreams of melancholy men, / I think and think on things impossible...' You must want to be *you*, Sled-boy, and then, if your want is sufficient, equal to, or stronger than the want of the people who have houses like this, you'll get yours."

"According to you, all you need is just to want something, Mr. Briard. I *want* all right. I'm plenty good in that department. What I need is money."

"No, Sled-boy. You only think you want money. Which is interchangeable with a house like this, etcetera. Perhaps you don't understand what I mean because I haven't said it comprehensibly. What I call want has also been called ambition—which Shakespeare decries again and again with soaring odium, or pluck, as Mrs. Tippet might call it, or dedication, as our artists have always looked upon it. Or, as Mr. Freud's flock sees it, 'sublimation and hostility.'

"Ben is doomed to be a successful actor simply because his want in that direction is as great, or greater in my opinion, than most of the wants in his generation. And, accident happens to be in his favor."

"What accident?" Ben said.

"That I'm your father. That I'm not successful."

"You're not?" Sled-boy said, perplexed, but no more so than Ben and me.

Ben spoke for both of us. "How do you mean, you're not?"

"Consider the history. It took me forty years to understand what I'm telling you now—to define the importance of want. It took me even longer, inexcusably longer, to find a direction for my want. A successful man is positive of his direction when he's your age, Ben. He's not so sure, in his twenties. He's even more doubtful in his thirties—and, at my age, he's reached whatever goal he set out for and is too busy enjoying it to spend precious time analyzing it."

"But you've reached a goal," I said. I couldn't have said what his goal was, but it hurt me to hear him say he was unsuccessful.

"Yeah. You got this house," Sled-boy said.

"That's no more a goal than money is. My want was the simplest and most popular one in the world—for a home and family. And that want became enormous, unbearably heavy. But it came late, and, as accident had it, too late. Or, it could be, I too, right now, am costuming fact as accident. Was my wife's death accidental? Or was it the result of both our greeds, our late-arriving, overwhelming wants?" He spoke without speaking to any of us, as though he forgot we were there.

"The human body is sometimes tragically impractical for human wants. We'd been told it was dangerous for her to have another child. But we couldn't make ourselves hear. Once, one feeble little once, I tried to talk to her about it...but she was so used to painting the world the colors she wanted it to be..."

"She could have stayed home," Aunt Catherine said in a tight voice.

"She couldn't have or she would have," my father responded bluntly, and he was aware of us all again. "So, Sled-boy. I have part of a family—and a house. I've had a couple of dozen houses. Don't worry about getting a house."

"To tell you the truth, Mr. Briard," Sled-boy said, "I *wasn't* worried about that when I came in here tonight. I was only worried about maybe somebody tipping off the police."

My father laughed. "That's a good, sensible worry, Sled-boy. Survival. You just keep worrying about surviving, and you'll get the house to worry about it in."

The light in the guest room went on. Aunt Catherine noticed too, her cheeks flushing. It went off, and we heard Frank's quick steps down the stairs. He danced into the room, a broad grin on his face, Aunt Catherine's black leather pocketbook dangling from one triumphantly upraised hand.

"Hey!" Ben cried in instantaneous protest.

"Know what happens to be in here?" Frank orated. "I'll happen to tell you." With exaggerated delicacy, he lowered and opened the pocketbook.

"Dear Lord, dear Lord," murmured Aunt Catherine.

"There happens to be...let's just looky see," said Frank, "two hankies with little flowers on the edge, one comb, two bottles of pills, a bunch of Kleenex, a bunch of keys, one bus ticket to Tulsa, Oklahoma—"

"Oh!" cried Aunt Catherine.

"Catherine!" said my father in an astonished tone. "What happened to the plane ticket? You *promised* this time."

She bit her lower lip.

"Where was I?" Frank said, in his mincing satire of impossibly good manners. "One bus ticket, a pair of ladies' stockings, a hair net, *and*, it just happens, eighty-seven dollars and fifty-six cents in this little zip-place!"

"This is outrageous," my father said calmly.

"Oh, Walter...I was going to tell you," Aunt Catherine said, blanching and starting to weep again.

I couldn't interpret that exchange right off. My first understanding was confused. Aunt Catherine never carried more than twenty dollars. She was certain any sum over twenty mystically magnetized thievery—which seemed to be the case here this evening. But how was it that she had trusted herself with eighty-seven? My father's "outrageous" clearly referred to Frank's or anyone's unallowed and blatant inspection of another's private property. Yet Aunt Catherine was apologetic to my father, rather than as incensed as my father at Frank's rank intrusion.

It wasn't until Ben, more loudly objecting than my father, yelled, "That's not fair. That's hers!" and Aunt Catherine sobbed, "No, Ben..." that I realized that the extra sixty-seven had been contributed by the airline company to whom she had returned my father's gift of a plane ticket—a gift which she'd accepted with effusive, nervous appreciation. Of course, the cheaper bus ticket was her real preference. In her present guilt and remorse at keeping the refunded money from the airline, obviously she thought "outrageous" referred to her embezzlement.

But all of this was lost on Ben. "Her money wasn't part of the bet," he said to Frank. "I bet that we—meaning the people that live in this house—didn't have more than what was in my pocket and my father's and Lucresse's four sixty-five anywhere in this house."

"You said 'in this house,'" Frank rebutted, his voice rising.

"Now wait a minute!" Sled-boy yelled at both of them.

"Take it; take it!" Aunt Catherine wailed.

"The bet was, if you found any more money than what's here and her four sixty-five of *ours*, in this house," Ben steamed.

"So I *found* more—in this house!" Frank hollered.

"Just a *minute!*" Sled-boy hollered back.

Frank and Ben held their breath. But given quiet, Sled-boy found his mind inhibited by forces more powerful than noise. Uncomfortably, he fell as silent as the ones he had silenced for his say.

"The problem is an enigma," my father said, seeming greatly pleased about it. "But then, *every* problem is, while it exists. Did Ben designate 'money in this house,' or, 'money belonging to people who dwell, currently, in this house'? What he actually said makes little difference. Did you, Sled-boy, and you, Frank, understand that he meant the money in this house, or, the money owned by the people who live in this house? *That* is of crucial importance. That makes this an issue of morality."

"We were talking about Briard money," Ben said.

"We were talking about money. Plain, ordinary money. Anybody's," Frank said.

"It would seem that we've come to an impasse," my father said. "This is why some people live as lawyers. So often, what was *understood* is *not* understood. Because nothing is ever fully said, you know. In fact, the more intelligent the people involved are, the less is usually said. In this case, for example, we all agree that it wasn't necessary to say, 'the money we have in this house precludes from the bet any monies in the Terters' place down the street or in the Third National Bank.' It was sufficient to say, 'in this house,' thereby, *ibidem*, limiting the bounds of the bet to funds, bullion, currency, specie, belonging in this house. Now comes the question of ethics. Does the money in Mrs. Tippet's purse belong in this house?"

"It was here," Frank said.

Sled-boy looked troubled. "But if it's a question of ethicalness, like Mr. Briard says, then it don't *belong* here, stupid."

"No, no, dear Sled-boy," my father reasoned. "I don't believe Frank is stupid. He merely wants to win the bet, for which I can't blame him. I love to win bets. But being an intelligent young man, I know he wants to understand whatever he does, thoroughly. Frank, did you come here with any previous knowledge of Mrs. Tippet's presence, or the presence of any of her possessions in this house?"

"No," said Frank uneasily.

"Only the Briards occupied this house, to your knowledge?"

"Yeah."

"You meant then to gather what you could from the Briards?"

"Yeah."

"Then certainly money belonging to Mrs. Tippet cannot be considered in this situation, as it was never understood to be considered, though that may not have been fully discussed—any more than money in the Third National Bank was discussed. It seems to me it was a fair bet. Had you found a hundred thousand dollars belonging to me or to Ben or to Lucresse, aside from her four dollars and sixty-five cents, it would have been yours to take."

"But—" Frank began.

"He's right." Sled-boy stood, gun in hand and facing Frank. He held out his other hand commandingly, and Frank gave him Aunt Catherine's pocketbook.

"But, Sled-boy," Frank groaned, "I couldn't *find* her four sixty-five! I think she was lying. And if she *was*, then what kind of a fair ethics bet was it anyways?"

"Where is it, Lucresse?" Ben asked.

"In my socks' drawer," I answered. "Rolled up in the red pair."

"Jeez," Frank said with disgust.

"That's typical of Lucresse," Ben said. "It's there all right. I'll show you."

He and Frank left the room together. Sled-boy gave a long-suffering sigh. "That guy really *is* stupid, Mr. Briard. Never can find anything. Never can imagine anything different from just exactly what you tell him to expect. This job tonight, it turned out a lot different from what I planned. If he was smart, you'd think he'd *know* that by now and knock off."

"'*Gang aft a-gley*,'" my father said.

"What?" said Sled-boy.

But Frank and Ben returned, Frank holding my sock. "It's in here, okay," he said miserably.

"So that ends the bet," Ben said. "You pay us four sixty-five."

"'The best-laid schemes o' mice an' men *gang aft a-gley'*—'often go astray,'" said my father. "Robert Burns. A superior romantic poet."

"Jeez," Frank said again, and dropped my sock on the lamp table.

Sled-boy laughed in a confident, patronizing way and put Aunt Catherine's pocketbook next to my sock. He took a bright tan, tooled leather wallet from his back pocket and extracted a bill. "Here's a five," he said, giving it to Ben. "Keep the change."

"Oh, that's not necessary," said Ben, risking hurting Sled-boy's pride in order to preserve his own.

"Ben!" said my father sharply. "You say thank you."

"Thanks, Sled-boy."

"That's okay. I guess it's getting late."

My father stood up and I did the same.

"It sure was nice meeting you, Mr. Briard," Sled-boy said. "I appreciate the talk we had."

My father guided him toward the front door, shaking his hand. Ben and Frank followed. Sled-boy's awkwardness in the protocol of departure was no more or less than many people's, only of shorter duration. And, considering the turn of the evening's events, this spoke well indeed for his taste and control.

"Funny how things happen," he said, waving Frank ahead of him through the door. "Who would have thought? What you said about success and all, Mr. Briard? And accident? Well, it sure was nice meeting you." He smiled to me and Aunt Catherine across the room. "Sorry if we disturbed you."

"Not at all," my father assured him.

Sled-boy about-turned and was gone into the dark.

My father closed the door after him, but almost before it clicked, Aunt Catherine sprang to her feet, flat palms against the sides of her head, her neck muscles rope-like in contraction. "I was afraid you were going to say, 'Come again!'" she whispered hysterically.

My father reached toward her with placating arms, but before he could touch her, she whirled into the den, and a moment later we heard her frantic cry into the telephone, "Operator! The police! Send the police! The Briard house, Maple Drive! Robbers! Send the police! Hurry!"

Then she sped back into the living room, straight to the lamp table, and grabbed her pocketbook. She examined its contents with knowing hands and passionate eyes.

"I suppose there was no point in asking you not to make that call, Catherine," my father said.

She looked up in surprise. "Walter! They were robbers!"

"But they didn't rob."

Ben laughed incredulously. "They lost five dollars."

"Ben, move the tapestry nearer the wall," my father instructed. "I don't want the *gens d'armes* trampling on it."

"Walter, they had a gun!" exclaimed Aunt Catherine.

"But they didn't shoot. No harm was done. And I'd just as soon not have any publicity about this." He took out his handkerchief from his shirt pocket, unfolded it carefully, and balanced the Peddicord diamond at its center in the palm of his hand.

"No, Walter!" gasped Aunt Catherine. "You didn't have that on you the whole time!"

"Yes, I did."

"Just think! They could have stolen *that!* And you say no harm was done."

"But in fact, it wasn't."

"It was attempted robbery, that's what it was," she cried, "and I never *will* understand *you!* Poor Jen!"

"Whether you understand me or not, I discount any attempt at robbery they made. It may have been an *intended* robbery, but not attempted, really. And I shall not press charges to the police. Do you understand that?"

"No, I don't. For the sake of these children, if you won't press charges against men who come here with a gun, I *will*."

My father looked suddenly tired. "Have you never had an evil thought, Catherine? Is it possible that you alone, among human animals, never entertained a malicious idea?" He let a purposeful glance fall on the pocketbook in her lap. "If every bad *intention* were to be reported to the police, they wouldn't have to investigate bad *acts*. Anyway, there is no such thing as justice against wicked intentions, and those who demand it are fools."

Aunt Catherine worked her hands inside her pocketbook. "Walter, there just wasn't time to tell you. It was only this morning that I..." She shuffled through the bills and counted off most of them.

"Forget that, Catherine."

"There just wasn't time. I *meant* to tell you," she pleaded, extending the money to him.

He waved her aside. "I have no idea what you're talking about now," he lied, concentrating on refolding his handkerchief around the jewel. "*I* was talking about the idiocy of trying to punish a man for evil intent. And how I won't do it. If it makes you feel better, one of the reasons I won't is that I don't want to invite any further visits from someone who may be more capable than Mr. Frank and Mr. Sled-boy."

"Do you think the police will bring reporters?" Ben asked.

"And photographers?" I added.

Aunt Catherine smoothed her hair.

"Maybe," my father said. "If the night man thinks the name Briard juicy enough."

"Listen, Dad," Ben said seriously. "I don't want my picture taken. Suppose, well, suppose when I'm playing Richard III or something like that, and it's a hit, you know, and the papers have this old picture of me in a story about something as silly as this? Well, I'd hate to have them dig it up *then*."

"Don't worry, Ben," my father said.

Aunt Catherine was smoothing the collar of her dress when the flashlights shone in the front windows.

There were four men: two in police uniform, armed; one in a gray suit, apparently unarmed—he was Detective Macci; and one young one, called Roley, lazily chewing gum. He carried a big camera with a flash attachment.

After matter-of-fact introductions, not nearly as cordial as our ones with the robbers—all of which Detective Macci seemed to be recording verbatim in a small notebook—my father expressed his regret that they had been summoned, that it was an unfortunate misunderstanding on Mrs. Tippet's part, that no crime had been committed, and that he had no charges to bring.

"But they *did* have a gun. *That's* why I called," Aunt Catherine interjected.

We all had to sit down with Detective Macci while the two uniforms wandered off, presumably to inspect the house. Roley rested himself and his equipment on the couch.

Detective Macci monotoned questions, which my father answered, providing more details of what had happened. He stressed the facts that the young men had rung the doorbell and that he himself had admitted them, and that while he couldn't be sure of what action they had originally intended—for, after all, how can one be sure of any other person's intentions?—what actually occurred was that he and they, separately and together, had a most pacific conversation, and that the young men left in the friendliest of moods—with nothing other than what they had brought with them.

I thought of saying "less five dollars," but I feared that would initiate a long explanation that my father would consider unnecessary. Also, I figured Detective Macci's writing hand must be getting tired. I know I sure was.

"So, you see," my father concluded, "this *was* a mistake. And I *am* sorry."

The two uniformed men weren't as light and swift as Frank, but they were more thorough searchers. They came back, each holding an arm of a still drugged, pajamaed, utterly confused Fred.

"Mr. Briard, Mr. Briard," he bleated, blinking manfully.

"It's all right, officers," my father said. "Fred is our houseman. Obviously there wasn't much excitement, or he couldn't have slept through it."

With his new pills and compulsion for sleep, Fred could have slept through a brass band's concert, but I kept my mouth shut.

"Mr. Briard," Fred whimpered, as the police unhanded him, "what *is* it?"

"Just a mistake, Fred," my father responded, signaling no more questions.

"It's just a job, with us," Detective Macci spoke in defense of the force.

"Of course," my father said with deep understanding.

Roley, on the couch, came to life. He stretched and adjusted his camera. "Might as well get a shot for the story though, huh? How 'bout everybody in front of the fireplace?"

Ben quickly retreated to the other end of the room, and I watched my father. Fred, still befuddled and appalled, watched him too. Aunt Catherine pressed the sides of her hair again, and said, "I look awful, but if you must have a picture..."

My father deterred her on the way to the mantel. "No, Catherine. There *is* no story."

"I was only trying to be cooperative."

He took her arm and led her into the den, talking to her in a low voice. At the same time, Roley took my arm and guided me to the hearth. "Just look natural," he said.

Surprised at being singled out and vaguely thrilled, I stood there as he crouched a few feet in front of me, his camera hiding his face.

A blinding flash blotted out everything, and in the coming-and-going pink, red, and purple that succeeded it, I distinguished Fred, staring dumbly at the rolled-up tapestry and carton, and Ben, intractable against the far wall, protecting his future notoriety. And as my sight returned, there was my father, emerging from the den with Aunt Catherine. He seemed refreshed, as though a taxing job had been completed. She followed a half step behind him, mute and submissive.

The next day's local newspaper printed my picture in the lower left corner of the second page, with the caption, *"Daughter of Walter Briard, well-known art dealer, whose home on Maple Drive was the scene of an intended robbery last night."* My father remarked they should have said "house."

I studied my photograph: my face had the same crazed smile preserved in our hundreds of snapshots of all my felonious birthday parties.

CHAPTER SEVEN: SEDUCTION AND LOSS

The tapestry didn't get unrolled and rehung until after we moved away from Palm Beach. For once, our move was almost part of a general exodus. Although we left three weeks before the official close of school—completing our grade requirements by some artful means I can no longer remember—our departure was almost in sync with several of my school chums, who had come there for the winter months and left as we did for their "real" homes in points north. We moved to a sizeable guesthouse on a large estate, twenty miles north of Chicago.

My father found entertainment to his liking there, mostly in the company of the elderly couple who owned the estate—people he had known forty years before in Europe. Ben found Toby Reiman and an amateur stock company there. And I found nothing but loneliness and discontent.

Even in late May, the wind off of Lake Michigan froze my bones. My father had dinner at the main house more often than at home. I wished Felicity was with us, but knew there wasn't a chance; freed from Mead, she had taken up residence in Mexico and was doing one "last" movie, which she had somehow managed to happily turn into a drawn-out affair. I felt I was too old to be seen anywhere with Fred, and there wasn't anyone else to accompany me to the activities available in "the loop." Ben was always busy with little, blonde, sixteen-year-old Toby, and she made me uncomfortable. Her energy and lack of inhibition made me feel dull and out of things. Every time she came into our house, she had to make a hurried, highly important phone call, which she accomplished in whispers. Or she needed a tissue, or a glass of water, or a safety pin—immediately. But she could sing with abandon—which she did at the slightest provocation—anywhere, and she let Ben and everyone else know that she judged him to have the greatest "talent" she had ever come across in her sophisticated, young life.

I'd endured one-and-a-half long months of invisibility and discontent when, as the temperature—and I—approached a broiling point, I came to a momentous insight: I knew what was wrong with me. I was almost fifteen, yet I still had not experienced a love affair!

I sat by the hour alone those still, hot days analyzing the problem, and by a form of self-hypnosis—the strongest persuasion there is—I began to envision myself as a vessel of incomparable sexual charm: a not-too-young, not-too-old legatee of Cleopatra's, Hedy Lamarr's, and Jane Russell's blatant sexuality. I was aware that in the myopic eyes of my father, Ben, Fred, and everyone who knew me, I seemed a slim, hardly developed girl, given to sudden childish laughter, whose principal interest lay in her habit of saying exactly what was on her mind, no matter how naïve or foolish it sounded. It would be difficult, if not impossible, to change that impression immediately. To do so, I simply had to find someone, a male, preferably attractive to me, who would accept the identity only I realized was my true self.

If you search diligently enough, you're likely to find a character with a particular necessary flaw. And though my territory was limited—the nearby tennis courts, the old garage that was the stock company's summer theater, the local movie house, coffee shop, and grocery stores—my purpose was obdurate and my intuition good.

The summer theater turned up a likely candidate in the person of

Arthur Frith. I almost dismissed him at first glance; he seemed too attractive to be a likely prospect. He was sixteen—older than Ben—taller and better built. His left eye was wide, innocent; his right smaller, crafty, roguish. But after I'd hung around the garage for a few days, where he was employing himself as prompter-stage manager-all-purpose assistant, for a production of *Harvey* in which Ben and Toby had roles, I knew that both his eyes were lies. He wasn't shrewd enough to be crafty or gentle enough to be guileless.

He was like a strong, slow animal that has just found out that it's strong and an animal. The director and the cast depended on him to do all the chores and ignored him when the chores were done. But he didn't mind when they went off in pairs and groups for a snack without him, nor did he sulk when they didn't include him in their conversations. This was because this summer theatrical was Arthur's first breath of freedom. From the moment he could remember, he had lived with his grandmother and her mother—accompanying, assisting, considering them. He'd never created any noise. The two old ladies, with grave compunctions no doubt, had gone to Minnesota for these summer weeks, and during the hiatus, Arthur had found he could be "Art" and useful to other people. I sensed that he was ready to be more than useful, to make a real impression on someone else. For instance, me.

One day after Ben and Toby and the others had left, and Arthur was methodically striking the improvised set, I approached him and realized almost instantly that it would take a good deal of effort to make him be impetuous; his old-lady background had all but precluded sudden desire.

"I'm Lucresse Briard," I said with the mysterious smile I'd been practicing. "Aren't you thirsty?"

"I have to get the chairs off," said Arthur, lugging a flat toward the back wall.

"I'll help you. Then we could go get something to drink."

"You don't have to." He put the flat down and looked at me uncomfortably.

I shrugged and sat down languorously on one of the chairs he would be removing in a moment. I stretched my arms above my head. "It's *so* hot for July. Much too hot to rush around the way those kids do. I like to move *slow*; don't you?"

Arthur shuffled over to me with his hands on his hips. "It's always hot in July," he said matter-of-factly.

"But what I think is most people don't know how to keep themselves cool. For instance, those kids—or maybe it's because they just aren't grown-up enough."

"I don't exactly understand what you're talking about."

I closed my eyes. I would be patient as well as alluring. "Lucresse, Arthur. Please address me by my name."

"Lucresse," he mumbled and shifted from one foot to the other.

"What I was thinking, Arthur, was, well, probably every one of those kids was dying for a drink about an hour ago, but they just had to go through the first act—practicing it over and over again—so they didn't get a drink when they were really thirsty. I believe in getting what you want *when* you want it."

"Oh." He smiled as though he wasn't sure he should smile—that it was the polite thing to do in this situation.

I smiled up at him as though he and I had shared an amusing joke. "Do you think Toby Reiman is attractive, Arthur?"

He studied his shoes. I could tell he had thought about her before. "She's all right."

"She sure jumps around a lot," I said, giving an offhand giggle. "Sometimes I wonder if she can hold still long enough for a kiss."

He shifted his weight and giggled too. "I wouldn't know."

"Well, certainly I wouldn't either—know, that is. Kissing is usually done in private. Anybody knows that."

"Yeah," agreed Arthur, his back straightening. "I have to take that chair you're on."

I could tell that it had now occurred to him that he and I were alone in the big garage. The first step on my journey to an affair had been accomplished!

The second and third were equally easy. Arthur accepted my suggestion that we go to the counter at the coffee shop, a place the others didn't frequent. And, his wide eyes narrowing with pride, he paid for my Coke.

Afterward, he walked me home. We walked side by side, two feet apart, and the more we walked, the more boyishly talkative he grew. That was when I learned that he lived with elderly women, and I suddenly feared that I was reverting to my false, unsophisticated self and was becoming his "friend." To recover my new self, I swung my hips a little.

"They say being a senior is tough," chatted Arthur. "But at least you're a *senior.* But you know what I worry about? After a whole year of being a senior—the tops—then you're nothing but a freshman again when you go to college."

I swung my hips even more. "I don't see that senior or freshman makes any difference. It's how you *feel* that counts. Why I've known *thirteen*-year-olds that knew more than college girls—about things that matter."

"How old are you, Lucresse?" he asked suddenly.

"Fifteen, practically," I answered nonchalantly.

"You sure know a lot for fifteen."

I felt like jumping up and down, but instead, I made my hips swing more subtly. "Enough. I know enough."

I put my hand in his. After a few steps, I was sorry. The picture of us that I was watching from somewhere out in space looked too much like youthful sweethearts. This was to be an "affair." Also, his hand was just a hand—like Ben's or Fred's. Its touch evoked no feeling other than skin on skin, indeed a rather unpleasant friction, both skins being sticky warm. I tried to withdraw my hand, but he held on. At my driveway, I yanked it away hard, at the same time trying to formulate the next thing to say, and a thought I'd never had before came to me: "Let's go down to the lake tonight for a moonlight swim," I suggested, resuming my languor.

Arthur's lips hardly moved. "That's a great idea."

"But you'll have to call me." Girls who had dates were called; Ben called Toby.

"Why?"

"To ask me," I said.

"But it was your idea."

"Even so." I raised and lowered one shoulder provocatively.

"All right. What time should I call?"

"About six," I directed. "My father and Ben should be home by then." This last sentence was a mistake and I knew it coming out of my mouth.

"But I don't want to call *them*!" he protested.

"Of course not, silly," I recovered. "It's just that I have to tell them I'm going."

"Oh." He hesitated a second's beat. "Do you have to tell them *everything?*"

"Everything I want them to know is all," I whispered, and then I smiled back at him sloe-eyed as I strolled into our house.

The phone rang at exactly six o'clock, and Ben got to it before I could. The male voice asking for me made him inquire in surprise: "Who's this?" Then he put the mouthpiece against his chest and glared at me. "It's Arthur Frith—for you. What does *he* want?"

I tore the telephone out of his grip. "I don't know yet."

I spoke in Toby's low, urgent way. "...Oh sure, Arthur. I'd love to. I'll be ready at seven thirty. Good-bye."

"You'll be ready for what?" asked my father, inspecting the framed East Indian batique scarf he had borrowed from his friends in the big house.

"To go swimming."

"Tonight?"

"With Arthur Frith?" Ben added.

"Yes. What's so amazing about that? He asked me for a date."

"That's amazing," Ben said.

"He's older than you," I retorted.

My father only half-listened as he searched the walls for space for his temporary acquisition. "These gods couldn't look more murderous in oil. Who is Arthur Frith?"

"He's the stage manager," Ben said. "A real slow, quiet kid."

"And the prompter," I said.

"Then at least he can read."

"Not very fast," Ben said.

"He's very deep. Ben hardly knows him."

"I know he's always losing the place."

"You're only picking on him because he asked me for a date."

Ben scratched his head. "I don't get *that* at all."

I made a nasty face at him. "I'm going to get undressed."

"Are you going to let her go, Dad?"

"I'm afraid this will have to hang in the kitchen," he answered on his way there. "But let's not tell Fred just yet. Lucresse hasn't asked me if she can go."

"I think she ought to *have* to ask you!" yelled Ben. "A little kid like her going off for a swim, with an older kid like Arthur, at *night!*"

"I'm not a little kid. Arthur doesn't think so, or he wouldn't have asked me. After all, he could have asked Toby Reiman, or anybody."

"Fat chance he'd have with her!"

"Now, now—that's all theoretical," my father jumped in, returning from the kitchen without the framed scarf. "Young Master Frith did not invite Toby, or anybody. He invited Lucresse."

"I *can* go, can't I? I already told him I would!"

"'May' you go," corrected my father.

"I may then, can't I? Please?"

"Of course you may, Lucresse," he said almost too sweetly. "You're an attractive young lady. Ben and I will have to get used to young men asking you for dates."

Somehow that—his acknowledgment of my dismal lack of experience in this area—made me feel less worldly than all of Ben's uncomplimentary remarks lumped together. "See?" I said to Ben weakly.

"Maybe I should go swimming tonight too," he said, to have the last say.

"No!" I yelled. "I don't go along when you go places with Toby!"

"Let me see...it must be thirty years since I went bathing at night," my father reminisced. "It was in Cannes, as I recall..."

"I never went out with you and Felicity either!" I said.

"I recall that very well. Felicity and I didn't go out."

"Even so," I begged, "you're not thinking of coming along with Arthur and me, or letting Ben come?"

"Oh, no. Of course not," he said. "I was only musing."

As I changed into my swimsuit, I thought of Jen with self-pitying love. Had she lived, this event wouldn't have been so agonizing. She would have been the end authority, would have dictated the attitude Ben and my father should assume. She would have pronounced a straight "Yes, you can go" or "No"—and bearing no resemblance to her sister Catherine, she more likely would have said "yes." Then the worst I would've had to face would have been the innocent, bothersome advice I'd heard that regular mothers usually gave.

But I had no mother. And more than anything now, I feared how my father and Ben might behave when Arthur came for me. First I hoped desperately that they would conceal their appraisal of my "new" role as a sought-after female. Then I hoped that, if they didn't conceal it, Arthur was slow enough to miss their insinuations—that I had no experience whatsoever and was "debuting" my new role with him tonight.

My fears and hopes were wasted. My father and Ben—undoubtedly because the former had advised the latter during my absence—were more deceitful than I could have wished. They shook hands with Arthur and mouthed innocuous remarks about how warm the night was and what a bright notion it was to go swimming. With just the right level of dispassionate sincerity, they wished us a good time, and we left.

Whereupon my confidence returned with a vengeance as Arthur and I walked the quarter mile through the dark, quiet streets to a path through someone's private property to the lake. The beachfront was deserted and iridescent under the moon. We could hear our feet slushing through the sand and the soft splash of the water. The sand was still warm from the day's sun, so I sat down on it and scooped great handfuls, letting it pour languorously through my fingers. Arthur stood, watching me.

"I've never come here before, like this," he said. "It's funny."

"How?" I dropped my chin so that I could look upward at him even more than was required by my sitting position beneath him on the sand.

"With nobody around—and no sun."

"Nobody to watch us."

"It's a funny feeling."

"I don't feel funny," I said. "I feel good."

"Let's go for a swim," he suggested. He offered me a hand, I grabbed it, letting him pull me to my feet, and we ran into the water, exchanging lilting laughs about how cold it felt.

"You have to move around." He swam a small, clumsy circle around me. I wished I liked him more. Even the way he swam was uninteresting. But he was sixteen and a boy. And he had to have noticed that I was a girl by now.

"I'm really cold," I called. "Let's get out."

Slowly, he followed me back to our towels on the sand. I hugged one around my shoulders, shivering perceptibly. "Sit down," I invited. "We can warm up together."

He dropped beside me, his bent left leg touching my right one. I moved my toweled shoulder under his armpit. He put his arm around me.

"You know, I think you're flirting with me," I said.

"Kind of, I guess." He moved his face to face mine. Then he moved it closer, until his two eyes, shining in the dim air, merged into one round hollow as I went cross-eyed. His arm on my shoulders tightened.

"Let's talk some more," I said, jerking my head to the other side.

He loosened his grip. "I sure had you all wrong."

"Why?" I was suddenly afraid that something had gone awry, and I had reverted to the status of the type of girl one doesn't flirt with.

"'Cause all along, at the place, you were so quiet and everything—I thought you were just Ben Briard's kid sister. I didn't think of you like *this*."

Relieved, I stretched out my legs straight in front of us, and crossed them at the ankles. "That was the impression I wanted to make. On purpose. After what I'd been through."

"How do you mean?"

"At the last place we lived, it was so sad..." I kept talking, while I tried to think of what I had been through. "You know, it's like most kids that haven't been through anything always try to look as if they have. People who've really been through things want to look as if they haven't."

"I guess I see what you mean," said Arthur. "What was the sad thing that happened where you lived before?"

"I don't really like to talk about it. It was an unhappy love affair. Several of them." I swallowed hard, as if to contain the pain.

"Gosh."

"Yes, one boy tried to commit suicide. He was a senior."

"You mean, because you didn't love him?"

"Well, I thought I did, for a while. But there were so many others. Of course, I'm over it all now. But I've made up my mind not to fall in love so quick again."

"I don't blame you."

"No matter how attractive a boy is."

"But you *are* over it. You sure?"

"Oh, positive."

He put his arm around me again. "Now you just want to have fun," he said throatily.

I stood abruptly, accidentally banging my elbow into his chest. "That's it. Now I just want to have fun!" I started running back into the water. "Last one in's a rotten egg!"

He galloped after me, and lunged at me, as I belly-whopped away from his outstretched hands, beneath the surface. I breathed in and swallowed at least a pint, and came up to see the shimmering outline of him, like a white walrus, zigzagging toward me fast.

I splattered to shore again, yelling, "I forgot how cold it was!"

He followed me out; his arms drooped despairingly at his sides. "It's not *that* cold."

"No?" I said between clenched teeth. "I must have caught a chill. Or maybe some disease. I hope it's not catching."

He stopped a yard away from me, his feet churning into the sand. "Gosh, I hope not, Lucresse. I really like you."

I picked up my towel and huddled in it again. "And I thought we'd have so much fun tonight."

"So did I," he said, despondent.

Felicity's expression, "*Oy gevalt*," went through my mind. If only he could say something less affable and dull than "so did I." I was convinced that he didn't understand the rules of the game I had invented especially for him—even though I myself was making them up as I went along. Had he been more perceptive, and experienced, at least in his imagination—which, after all, even Ben said I excelled at—we'd have been transported partners in lovemaking by now. Had it rained, drenching us in our closeness, had a police car's spotlight then exposed us with elongated shadows across the beach, there would be an excuse for his acquiescence to the idea of a disease. As it was, he had failed me.

"The best laid plans..." I said philosophically, misquoting one of my father's favorite poets. "I'd better go home now."

When we got to my house, all the lights were on in the living room, and I stopped Arthur at the driveway. "I feel better now," I said brightly. "And it's still early. Let's take a walk around the block and let our swimsuits dry more."

"If you want...if you're sure you're all right."

"Some people say the best thing for a chilly dizzy spell is to keep moving," I took him by the arm and walked briskly away from the house.

"Were you dizzy, too?"

"Just for a minute. I'm fine now. Really."

"But maybe..."

"It's just that I'm more sensitive than most people," I said quickly.

"To what?"

"To everything." I pulled his arm around my waist and kept in step with his jerky stride. "To night air, and everything."

I walked him around the block once, and then around the one in the opposite direction, making a figure-eight hike. I told him he walked very well and that most boys as young as he didn't appreciate the appeal of walking well. And I figured another half hour had gone by.

At our driveway, for the third time, he put his free hand at the other side of my waist and said, "I really like you, Lucresse."

"Then you'll call me tomorrow, to see how I feel."

"But you said you were all right."

"You'll call anyway," I said, determined.

"If you want me to."

I left him and went in. The lights, still shining, were illuminating a game of two-handed solitaire with one kibitzer. My father and Ben were the players; Fred was watching. None of them knew who was winning. I knew they were waiting for me. Ben stared at me angrily.

"Did you have a nice time?" my father and Fred asked in one voice.

"Oh, very nice. I hope you weren't waiting up for me. I might have been much later."

"Where did you and the deep Arthur go?" Ben demanded.

"Swimming, of course. He's a wonderful swimmer," I said with a mysterious smile.

"I took a walk down by the beach not more than a half hour ago, and you weren't there," Ben said.

"*We* took a walk, too, after we were through swimming. Daddy, how could you let him try to spy on me that way?"

"I wouldn't order either one of you *not* to take a walk," my father said innocently. "I'm glad you had a nice time, Lucresse."

"It's not fair. And he better not do it again!"

"Oh, do you have another date with deep Arthur?" said Ben sarcastically.

"Naturally. He'll be calling me tomorrow. You'll see."

"Oh, dear," Fred said to my father, who said nothing.

"And I have no idea where we'll be going or what we'll be doing," I continued. "So nobody needs to follow me or wait up for me." I turned on my heel to go to my room.

"Lucresse!" snapped my father.

I stopped—stricken with the thought that my new woman-of-the-world career was about to be cut short long before its prime.

"Nobody needs to follow you or wait up for you, if you remember one thing."

"What?"

"What I told you before. That you're a *very* attractive young lady."

"Oh, that," I quipped. "Sure." And suddenly I resented him more than I did Ben. Ben didn't think I was attractive and was only attempting to interfere in my life and dominate me. If my father *did* think I was attractive, why wasn't he trying to protect me from the ravishing impulses of the Arthurs and Georges and God-knows-who-elses he believed would be pursuing me? Why wasn't he *there* for me, supporting me and giving me rules and...

I went to my room, determining that it would take several more dates, and much more adultlike serenity about them on my part, to gain my objective. A family of males—dominating or unprotective as they may be—was no blessing to a female intent on magnetizing the attention of other males—males who would value her for who she really was.

Sometimes, when chasing, the chaser gets carried away with his own momentum and doesn't notice when the chased stops running. The chaser passes, the chased starts up again, and the chaser finds that he is the chased. Usually, the original chaser is not aware of the exchange—any more than I realized the exchange of initiative when Arthur called me the next day. I thought he was simply following my suggestion to the letter.

That afternoon, and for several subsequent evenings, we talked a mutually exciting romance during aimless walks, over Cokes, in the emptied playhouse. I drew as near as possible to him as often as possible, but became bored and petulant when his arm would tighten about my waist. Twice he became breathless and inarticulate, both times stammering, "But I really like you, Lucresse." "Yes," I would agree, tenderly pushing him away, and answering, with no explanation for the push, "and I like you too, Arthur."

Though I came home early each of the evenings, my father, Fred, and Ben took care not to be caught waiting for me. Never had they regularly retired so early. A light was left on for me in the living room, and no one asked me any questions other than the familiar "Did-you-have-a-good-time?" In the morning, Ben even ceased referring to Arthur, who called daily, as "the deep." I had arrived; my private image of myself had become a reality to them so fast. Would Jen have been so trusting of, or indifferent to, my continence?

The manager of the neighborhood movie house had devised a weekly Saturday night event that had met with wide acceptance among the high school population, not including Ben—a midnight showing of the current film. I had never attended one; it was strictly and especially an attraction for dating pairs. Ben had gone a couple of times and didn't see that the late hour of the showing made the movie shown any more absorbing. Nevertheless, because Toby wanted to, he was going again this Saturday midnight.

"I want to too," I said. "I'll speak to Arthur about it."

"I don't know if they let fourteen-year-olds in," Ben said.

"They'll let me in, if I'm with Arthur."

"She wouldn't be home until two thirty," Ben explained to my father, totally demolishing the wall of reserve he'd retired behind concerning my recent activities.

"That *is* late," my father said.

"But if it doesn't make the picture any different, why should it make my going out any different?" I reasoned.

My father gave his approval, with a suggestion that bordered on an order. "But I suggest that you come home immediately after the show."

Ben left to get Toby before Arthur came to get me, and at the theater, I made certain that our seats were as far away from theirs as choice permitted. I didn't see Ben again until the show was over and we were all emerging. Then he approached us, with Toby tagging along, holding his hand. Quickly, I took Arthur's hand and riveted my attention to the framed stills in the lobby.

I heard Ben and Arthur exchange hellos, and Ben tapped me between the shoulder blades, hard.

"Oh, hello!" I said in surprise.

"Did you like it?" he asked.

The picture had been about a very poor, beautiful maid (Loretta Young—uniforms by Adrian) who falls in love with the very rich, handsome son of her employers (Robert Taylor—referred to three times by other characters as "the scion of a wealthy industrialist") and the difficulties (there were four of them) they have in readjusting their social inequality. The theme of the vehicle was that Robert Taylor photographed very well smiling, but that Loretta Young looked best smiling through tears.

"Oh, I thought it was great," I said.

"You would."

"Let's go get something to eat," Toby said.

"Lucresse has to get home."

"Arthur and I have to meet somebody first," I said.

Toby yanked Ben's hand. "I want some chili."

"Who do you have to meet?" Ben probed.

"Nobody you know." I pulled Arthur into a fast walk. "See you later," I called from the sidewalk.

"G'bye," Arthur called weakly as I hurried him on. "Where are we going?"

"I don't know. But I am not going home right now just because he says so. After all, he's only my brother and we're practically twins."

"He sure does get snotty sometimes. I've noticed that at rehearsals. He's pretty good at acting though."

"Snotty, that's what he is."

Arthur put his arm around me. "You're nice."

"Thank you."

"I only have four cents left. The tickets got my last buck for this week."

"So?"

"So the old lady's letter, with dough, won't come till Monday—if she remembers. She's so old she keeps forgetting things. Especially about money that's coming to me. She says she's saving it for me by saving it *from* me."

"What for?"

"Oh, college, I guess. And so's I'll have dough in my old age, like her and her mother."

"That's a long time. I can have all the money I want. All I have to do is ask Fred. He works for us, and he and my father are real old too. But not like your grandmother and her mother. They let me do practically anything I want. Which is swell."

"Do you have any money with you now?"

"No."

"Gee, that's a shame. We could've gone somewhere to eat too."

"Yes, it's a shame."

"I know where. Let's go!" he said like a slow explosion that had been contained for a long, long time.

"Where?"

"To *my* house! There's food. And nobody's there!"

We hurried. Arthur, because having an idea of his accepted, or, just having an idea, seemed to invigorate him. I, because the idea provided a temporary needed refuge, ensuring that I wouldn't be home before Ben.

Sitting in Arthur's kitchen, we fixed ham and cheese sandwiches. Arthur gulped his. I nibbled, chewing very slowly to let as much time go by as I could. I made eating take twenty minutes by Arthur's grandmother's mother's kitchen clock, and the slower the seconds seemed to tick, the less point there was to being there at all. I was tired and couldn't think of anything to talk about.

"I guess I'd better go home now," I finally said dejectedly.

Arthur's face grew dark. He stood up and came over to me. Standing in front of me, he put his hands on my shoulders and pushed his face very close to mine. "We didn't come here just to *eat*," he said emphatically. "I *told* you, nobody is here..."

His face, above mine and bearing down on me, frightened me. His fingers began to hurt at the nobs of my shoulders. "I want to go home," I said with a sudden burst of spirit.

He took one step back and allowed me stand up. Backward, I moved, until the door of the icebox stopped me. He followed and caged me against it on either side of my neck, his big hands flat against the icebox door. His eyes—both of them—were bright with anger as he drew near me again. "I've tried every which way to be nice," he said breathily. "But you don't act as if you like me."

"*I* like you, Arthur." My new voice was almost-adult, but in that mysterious place behind my eyes, the place where Felicity had once seen me, the place that I worked so hard to hide—even from myself—the place that had dropped into my stomach like a stone the night of the robbery about a million years ago, another voice was screaming: "Get out *now!*"

As Arthur moved in further, his nose bent into my cheek, banging my head back into the solid icebox door. His mouth on mine was stiff as his jawbone, and though the voice in my head was roaring, I couldn't make a sound...because I couldn't breathe. The furious kiss seemed never-ending. I tried to think. I wondered if he could breathe.

For a second, I couldn't remember who he was. But then I remembered, and I didn't want to hit him or kick him, but I didn't want to suffocate to death even more. As the voice in my head went silent, all thinking ceased, and it was like my brain was in my body instead of my head. In one fast motion, I bent both knees sharply, dipping into a stooped position, and scuttled under the bridge of his left arm. His pressing-forward head slammed into the door and he let out a cry like a huge, wounded animal.

"I'm sorry," I gasped from the kitchen doorway. "Really, I didn't mean..."

But it was as if he didn't hear me. Because this wasn't Arthur. It was that big animal I'd sensed when I'd first seen him. This big, stupid, unimpetuous animal that I'd tamed and trained to my whim now prowled toward me as I backed into another room. This animal held one hand to its forehead as it approached, and there were tears in its eyes. I knew that both his head and his feelings were hurt, but I didn't care. Where was I? It was the living room. Without taking my eyes off him, I sensed for an outside door.

"'Call me at six; call me tonight; we'll take a walk,'" he said in a hurt, mimicking tone. "You've fooled around with me long enough! Everybody always thinks they can tell me what to do. Well, they can't!" he nearly sobbed.

There was a door—I'd found it through my peripheral vision—and it was wide. It was off a narrow hall off the far end of the living room. I backed in its direction and bumped into the arm of an old-fashioned sofa. I spoke slowly, as though he had difficulty understanding English. "I don't want to tell you what to do, Arthur. I only told you what *I* wanted to do. And I want to go home now. That's all."

"But for once we're going to do what *I* want first," he said, still coming toward me.

"Arthur!" I shouted, surprising even myself. "Do you really think Ben is a good actor?"

If he heard what I said he might have asked "Who's Ben?" or "What's an actor?" in his immediate, animal state. But he didn't hear and he didn't say anything. He just kept coming, his crafty eye and his guileless one achieving the same expression—driven, purposeful, blazing—focused on me.

"Arthur!" I yelled again. "I didn't tell you the truth about that boy who tried to commit suicide—he didn't. My father almost killed him, that's what really happened. My father has a terrible temper."

"That kid should've killed *you*, that's what *should* have happened," he growled.

Whirling away from the sofa, I dashed down the hall for the wide door, threw it open, and gasped. It was a dark, musty-smelling closet! There was another narrower door with four glass panes in its upper half on the opposite wall that couldn't be seen from the living room. I leapt for it, but simultaneously Arthur leapt at me. We clashed just as I clutched the door's brass knob.

How often in my life I'd felt like hitting someone, but I never did—except with Ben. When we were much younger, now and then one of us took a swat at the other and initiated a wrestling match. But those erratic explosions were governed by an unwritten, undiscussed set of rules: the one on his (or generally, her) back was the defeated and the opponent ceased and desisted; we could not cry for help or Fred would scurry to the scene and stop the battle, which imposed a measure of self-control on each assailant not to injure the other too severely. And after the first propelling anger had dissipated, either party could end the fight at any time by the traditional declaration, "I give up," or the same idea camouflaged as a suggestion of something else to do.

Here, now, in this narrow hallway, there were no rules and no cry for help would be heard by anyone. As Arthur grabbed my left arm near the elbow with his right hand and pulled me away from the door, the animal that was me seized his swinging left hand with my right, shoved it in my mouth and bit into the soft cushion of the upper palm with the grip of an alligator.

A prolonged animal "Iuhh-uhh!" erupted out of his throat as his grip on my arm weakened. I bit deeper still. I bit till my upper and lower teeth were no more than a bone apart and I could taste the warm salt of blood. Only then, I released the hand, punched both my fists into the middle of his torso, causing him to lurch back, cradling his bleeding hand in front of his nose as he tried to examine it. His eyebrows were high, surprised, unbelieving. Funny almost—like that first appearance of puppet robbers or Aunt Catherine confronting lies or maybe me when I decided to be a woman of the world.

Despite his suddenly human response, I wasn't sure the mind behind the eyes was in operating shape again, and I yanked open the door and slammed it closed from the outside.

"Soak it in cold water!" I yelled. "My father has a worse temper than mine!" And I broke into a gallop in the direction of the estate.

"Iuhh-uhh-ohhh," he called back. "I hate you!"

Halfway to our house, I dropped to a jogging trot, slowed less by breathlessness than by an overwhelming a sense of failure. In the movies, the heroines resisted inevitable attacks on their virtue with a light slap on the face. They didn't resort to references to their fathers or brothers. They didn't get into fist fights and try to bite somebody's hand off. A femme fatale should be capable of paralyzing an army with the lift of one disapproving eyebrow.

The night, three thirty in the morning, was black-dark, warm, and breezy. Each breeze sent shivers through me, and as I mourned my failure as a seductress, I gradually lost all touch with the mysterious place behind my eyes that, knowing the truth of what had almost happened, had roared.

All the lights were on in our living room—I could see them from a block away. Utter hopelessness retarded my steps as I tried to choose between the explanations that came to mind as to where I'd been and what I'd been doing during the last hour. I couldn't explain to myself how an affair that was intended to have something to do with love had turned out more to do with murder, so I forgot about it. Then I braced myself to face my father's quiet interrogation and Ben's righteous indignation.

No one was in the lighted front rooms when I entered our house. Voices, muttering low, urgent, broken-off phrases, incomprehensible, but alarming in their tones, and a sound of strangled moaning that was even more alarming were coming from the back.

I swept through the kitchen to the full view through Fred's open door: all three of the men in my life were in a position so foreign to any I could have imagined that for a wavering second, I almost laughed. My father, Fred, and Ben were all in their pajamas. My father was sitting on Fred's bed, holding Fred on his lap, rocking him to and fro as if he were a baby.

Fred's glasses weren't on. His hands were clasped together, and shaking, in his own lap. His bare feet dangled and kicked spasmodically, in rhythm with the motion of the rocking.

Ben, kneeling before them by the side of the bed, was trying to catch one foot, then the other, and when he was successful, he rubbed the pale, white skin with his hands with a circular movement.

"Hold on, hold on," was what my father was saying in a sing-song chant as he swung Fred backward and forward.

It was Fred who was moaning, also in rhythm with the rocking. At the end of each moan, he said, clearly, "Hold me; hold me."

My father held him tighter. The rocking, the moaning, the rubbing, the repeated plea, went on for another minute as I stood stricken and hardly breathing at the doorway.

Once Ben looked up, straight at me, without pausing in his massaging, and didn't appear to care that I was there or not.

As I watched, Fred's clasped hands flew apart with force enough to undo my father's protective arms and Ben's grasp on one foot, and Fred fell to the floor. He gasped once with a great tremor, seemed to hold his breath for an elongated moment, and finally breathed again quietly.

What I remember after that is disconnected, the way only brilliant fragments are recalled out of a long nightmare. A man with a doctor's satchel came. Without asking who he was, I led him back to Fred's room. He spent a long time in there. He told us that Fred was to be moved to a hospital and he made a telephone call. Two other men arrived and carried Fred out of the house on a stretcher; they didn't bump into a wall or a doorframe on the way out. My father followed them, leaving Ben and me by ourselves. We waited and waited, not speaking to each other very much. And when we did speak, it was with the cool politeness of strangers.

It had been daylight for quite some time when my father returned. He looked tired, but unmistakably happy.

"It was a bad attack," he said with an incomprehensible smile. "But it was lucky. A warning. He's going to be all right."

"When? When will he be back?" we wanted to know.

My father's smile disappeared. "He needs several weeks of complete rest—then, partial rest. He *won't* be back—with *us*."

Before Ben or I could question this, he said emphatically, "But the point is, he's going to be all right. The doctor assured me. He'll have to go home..."

"Home?" I cried. Fred's home was our home.

"To his maiden cousin in Wales," said my father. "His destination every time he threatened to leave all these years." My father smiled again. "But you should have heard the protest he put up when he heard the doctor and me talking about it. Even under sedation, he made a frightful squeal. When I realized what he was thinking, I said, 'Fred, you know you won't rest with *us*. Would you rather take a chance on dying?'

"He said, 'I might die, sir. That's what I think.' I said, 'But not soon, if you go to your cousin's.' Nevertheless, the son-of-a-gun insisted that I look over his will."

With us trailing along, my father took an old leather briefcase from Fred's closet, brought it to the dining room table, and opened it. From it, he withdrew a thin letter and three large, brown paper envelopes.

One contained a clipped-together stack of French francs. Another had a bunch of United Kingdom pound notes. The fattest held a thick stack of pre-war German marks. My father didn't add them up. "He never did believe we weren't going back," he commented as he unfolded the letter. It was dated ten years before, and he read it to us. (I have it on my desk now.)

The last Will and Testament of Frederick Straun Holly. I hereby bequeath all monies to be divided equally between my cousin, Elizabeth Holly Hooks, Benjamin Briard, and Lucresse Briard. All personal effects to same. Except for my chauffeur's habit, including visored cap, in which it is my wish that my body be dressed for burial. It is my earnest desire that the site of said burial be beside the grave of Mr. Walter Briard, wherever that may be, if such is at all possible...

My father looked up in astonishment. "Why...he always assumed that I'd go first! The son-of-a-gun!"

"Is Fred younger than you?" Ben asked.

"He'd never say. But I think he's three or four years older." My father resumed reading.

...At the time of my demise, should the remains of the aforementioned Mr. Walter Briard have been cremated, as Mr. Briard has voiced a preference for rather than for a decent burial, I herein implore those in concern to please try to arrange a resting place for me in a cemetery near the scene of said cremation. I humbly suggest, in such circumstances, that a clergyman of any faith might be of assistance, even though one with whom my legatees (herein named) have had no previous contact may

prove to be a bit sticky. Therefore, I beg that they consider this second suggestion—that they offer the available man of the cloth whatever monetary gratuity necessary, to be taken from the monies of my estate, for the accomplishment of said service.

"Ho!" my father exploded, and we all burst out laughing.

We laughed until Ben lay across the table, heaving, and my father held his head in his hands. I doubled up on my chair, my knees pressed into my chest as my laughter became painful.

Then, all at once, though the pain didn't stop, I wasn't laughing anymore. I was crying. "But Fred *isn't* going to die, is he?" I sobbed.

"No," my father consoled me, not laughing anymore either. "Not for many years, I hope—if he spends them quietly at Miss Hooks's."

There seemed no reason to cry, and nothing we could say. Though we were trying, none of us could imagine life without Fred.

CHAPTER EIGHT: PASSAGE

The maid from the big house came in to clean ours and cook our meals during what felt like weeks that Fred was in the hospital. Her food was too neat and skimpy compared to his. We felt that our eating inflicted a willful injustice on the woman.

Fred was released—thinner, paler, resigned to the future the doctor decreed for him.

My father announced plans in a charged, determined manner. He could no longer take his time with individual clients. He wanted to be available to as many of them as possible at the same time. New York was the capital of the art objects world—he knew many people there—he didn't know why we hadn't gone there to live years before. On the telephone, he bought a house overlooking the Hudson River, forty miles north of the city.

He and Ben, and he and Fred had nagging arguments about the car. Ben wanted to take Fred's place at the wheel for the trip. Fred wanted to take his own place. And my father said he'd sooner learn to drive himself in the next few days than trust either one of them to get us and his velvet-lined satchel to New York.

Fred gave in, Ben fumed, and my father donated the old Buick to his friends in the big house—to use, sell, or junk—and he bought train tickets. The funny thing was, we all really wanted to fly, but we knew we'd have more time together on the train.

Once again, everything in the house was packed. But there was a difference this time that disturbed my usual detached equanimity about the proceedings: all Fred's belongings, including his old leather briefcase and its contents, were going with him on the train, and from it to a ship, to cross the Atlantic. And he wouldn't be with us at the new house to oversee the unpacking of everything else.

On the way to the railroad station, packed into a taxi, we passed Arthur Frith's house. His two elderly supervisors must have come home, for he was sweeping the flagstone path in front, the one that had served as my escape route the night of Fred's, and my, attacks. Arthur glanced up and, involuntarily, I waved to him. He did not wave back.

My glance shifted to Fred, in front with the driver, and I burst into tears. "I don't know why...don't know how...it'll be..." I whispered helplessly to my father.

"No one knows how life will be," he said. And, as Ben turned around inquisitively from the jump seat, "There's no rehearsal for living—or leaving."

CHAPTER NINE: WINDING HILL

When anyone asks me where I'm from, to save time, and because we lived there the longest, I say Winding Hill. Only once has anyone asked me what it was like there—a dreamy taxi driver in Milan when I was in my late twenties. To save time, again, since I was in a hurry to get to whatever was next—in that instance, the airport—I quipped that it was just a really old river town. "Ah," he said, "like Firenze."

Winding Hill was nothing like Firenze. There were differences—differences between Winding Hill and all the other places we'd lived. In ways, Winding Hill was the queerest, among civic anomalies. It was a carefully preserved residential oasis sprawling across the hills between two small, heavily industrial towns to its north and south. From almost any acre of it, you could see the river; the richer the householder, the higher on a hill was his house, and the more of the river he could see.

It was a worried community. The citizens worried about real estate developers attempting to buy large tracts from the estates of deceased Winding Hillers and putting up twenty-of-a-kind contemporary structures among the half-century-old houses. They worried about getting to the train to Manhattan in the mornings; morose husbands were sped to the station by tense-faced wives in a matinal ritual that made narrow, treacherous Winding Hill Road look like a speedway from its top to its bottom where it merged into the station platform at the river's edge.

They worried about what they called the "new people"—residents of fewer than ten years, some of whom had built houses with inch-thick fieldstone facades meant to resemble the older fortress-like houses, and others who bought old places through the executors of former occupants' estates. Those houses were still referred to by the names of the original owners.

We had the "Welch" house, which we rechristened the "noisy" house. Our name was a triumph of accuracy. Fifteen minutes after we arrived, we understood why, though it had been on the market for several years, no prospective buyer who had seen it had purchased it until my father told a realtor on the telephone that he'd take it, sight unseen—and, as it happened, unheard—provided we could move in immediately.

It was a stark, square, white stone building with twenty rooms—ten huge and ten tiny—set on a plateau halfway up Winding Hill Road, like an enormous headstone. Happily, its neighbors were all more than three acres removed. For there wasn't a faucet one could turn on without an ear-shattering response from the innards. A quarter-turn brought a harsh, low growl accompanied by a shrill wheeze that went up and up until its hissing decibels mercifully escaped the human ear. A full revolution provoked a violent crescendoing choking, clanging, and beating coughing spell, suggestive of a pair of armies clashing in medieval warfare. The flush of a toilet produced an even fiercer riot; it made one imagine that the implacable granite exterior walls were about to collapse. All the doors scraped or wheezed or whistled or squeaked; the kitchen's outside screen door was an odd one—it howled and squealed pathetically on the out-swing, but closed without so much as a whisper.

Rarely was there a quiet moment once we moved in, and the series of cleaning women and part-time cooks who passed in and out within the space of two weeks was dizzying. These people were distinctly individual souls with only one characteristic in common: they were all, for different reasons, unqualified to fill Fred's shoes. My father began to appreciate Fred's abilities more than he ever had before.

One woman, Tenny, had a mental block against laundry. She disappeared after my father found all of his shirts, abandoned in a heap, tied together by one shirt's sleeves and apparently hurled down the steps to the dank, dark cellar. Agnes was a stickler for routine; for her three-day tenure, she put dinner on the table at seven o'clock sharp whether my father was ready to eat or not. Mrs. Saalig was a brooding type who insisted upon being called Mrs. Saalig, which would have been quite all right except that she also insisted upon calling my father Walter and making the living room her salon in which she entertained him during her two days of service while the dinners burned. Mrs. Bellamy, who came and left just as swiftly, enjoyed an austere prejudice against food in general. Fresh fruit and vegetables were "contaminated," fowl and desserts were too fattening. Acceptable (to us) portions of anything acceptable (to her) were bad for the stomach juices.

At this same time, my father and I took turns answering Aunt Catherine's sudden and uncustomary flurry of correspondence. Ben disqualified himself from this duty by insisting he might say the wrong thing to her. Before we left Chicago, my father had informed her of Fred's attack and departure, and her first letter was waiting for us when we arrived in Winding Hill. In increasingly hysterical handwriting, she explained that she only wished she were "free to come keep house for you all, now that you don't have somebody to keep things going right the way they should be for growing youngsters anymore." This was followed the next week by a second letter, apparently mailed the day after the first, nearly screaming her remorse at our dire situation. Since my father had responded to the first letter, at my turn, I filled three pages, in larger than my normal handwriting, by telling her not to worry, I *loved* Winding Hill, (I didn't dislike it as I had our Chicago suburb, so that didn't seem too sizable an exaggeration), that I had made new friends again, (not really an *"L-I-E"* because school was to start in a few weeks, and I would have the opportunity to do so), and Tenny and Agnes and Mrs. Saalig and Mrs. Bellamy took up a page and a half. I was just being informative, but it seems my descriptions fanned Aunt Catherine's fears even more, and her third response was a long telegram announcing that if there was one thing about her that was a true fact, it was that she knew where her duty lay, she had always been the more responsible of Jen and herself, and that she would arrive the following Thursday to help set our new house in order.

I hadn't realized the change that had come over my father until he greeted this news with, "Good. Catherine has better sense than I do about some things."

"Aunt *Catherine*?" Ben said.

"Yes, and don't you forget it."

In the following days, I began to watch him, pay closer attention to the things he was doing, as if he were a puzzle I'd thought I'd known how to solve but suddenly found was still perplexing.

Most of the time, he wore the same sullen look as the men being hurtled to the eight twenty-six each morning. He spent whole mornings cleaning his desk. In a curt, thoroughly executive manner, he called an employment agency and commanded they supply yet another household worker—a man this time, who could oversee all his affairs, one who preferably didn't talk too much, and who could hire capable people for the various chores who didn't talk too much either. He didn't care what he'd have to pay him.

Hubert Peterman, former manager of a country club dining room, having struck out and failed in his own catering service, arrived. There was never a less aggressive, more inaudible, man who wasn't dead. Hubert was a widower of fifteen years, who was content to act out the stereotype fixed in his mind of what sort of person a widower should be. He came equipped with an old photograph album which he told me was his diversion in the evenings, when he was used to "sitting and reminiscing." By his second day, he had hired a maid away from the club who, in a silent trance of consideration for his widowerhood, did our cleaning and laundry. He did the ordering by telephone, softly, and cooked, if uninspiredly, to my father's order of "use lots of butter, and there's hardly anything we don't like."

Except for the paintings and tapestries that hung on most of the walls, most of the odds and ends of my father's collection began to disappear from sight. My father thought Hubert ideal for us, and quickly began to disappear into long silences very like his. He didn't seem to look forward to anything except Aunt Catherine's visit.

Once, Ben asked him for the third time if he could try out his new interpretation of Hamlet on him, and my father answered listlessly, "All right. But if it's as tumultuous as I think it's going to be, don't practice it when Catherine comes. You know Shakespeare isn't her greatest interest."

Ben paused. "When are you going to look up all the people you know here?" Usually by this time, three-and-a-half weeks after moving into a new residence, he was disappearing daily for meetings with people we never met.

"When we're settled."

"He's getting creepy," Ben said to me privately.

"Oh, I don't know." I didn't like having to agree with him.

"Then why is he so glad Aunt Catherine is coming? And this guy Hubert is like a ghost. I'll be glad when school starts."

"Me, too. Ben, I wish Fred was here."

"Don't say that to *him*."

The next morning, my father went out to the airport to meet Aunt

Catherine and escort her back. "Remember, I want you to do everything you can to please her," he warned us on his way out. "You don't see your aunt very often."

After he left, Ben gave orders. No one was to turn on a faucet or flush a toilet for the first half hour she was here.

"What happens if she has to go to the bathroom?" I said.

"You leave the room with her and break the news to her gently beforehand."

We didn't know why we were doing it, but following my father's lead, from the moment of her arrival early that afternoon, we paid court to Aunt Catherine. In response, she blossomed with good cheer and hearty conversation, told us seemingly endless anecdotes of doings in the retail drugstore business and the inside information about the rummage sale her church's Ladies' Guild held recently. She said she'd never seen a house of ours look neater and gave effusive credit to my father's good judgment in engaging Hubert. She said "that it *was* a shame about Alfred."

"Alfred?" we all said at once.

"Dear me! Fred, of course! It's just that every time I think the name Fred, I think of our Alfred Judd at home. He's always called Fred too, but *I've* always called him by his real name, Alfred."

My father nodded understandingly. I couldn't understand why her mistake didn't pierce his heart as it did mine. Fred was Fred, and how could anyone refer to him as Alfred? Who knows where he even was now, out in the middle of an ocean on a slow ship to a place I'd only read about in books! How dare she call him Alfred? But my father didn't seem the least wounded, not even pricked.

"Catherine, how long can you stay?" he said. "We have many things to talk about."

She said she could stay five days, and during those days, my father didn't deviate from the "things" he wanted to discuss. There was actually only one—the eventuality of his own death. His remarks and questions, and certainly their answers, demanded that Ben and I interrupt at times, but he wouldn't permit it. We listened to my father and Aunt Catherine's incessant conversations, staggered by the change in his attitude.

"...you do have an unusual sense of responsibility, Catherine—infinitely stronger than Jen's was..." As though Jen had been frivolously irresponsible in dying, as Aunt Catherine had so often implied.

"...as you know, there are many people I could appoint as their guardian, but..."

"...But after all, Walter, who would *care* as much as a blood relative?"

"Exactly my point, Catherine. Naturally, I hope Lucresse will be of age at the time, but if she isn't..."

"Walter, you know you can count on me to take care of them."

"There'll be money, and goods. You won't have to worry about the financial aspect of it..."

"Oh, I *thought* so, Walter! With all the stuff you have—and one thing I must say, Walter Briard always took care of his children *financially*!" She was already talking of him in the past tense!

Another time—

"...you're sure Joe wouldn't mind if they stay with you during vacations from school?"

"Why, of course not, Walter! When I think of all these years, with me coming to visit you, and not once you all staying over with *us*..."

He told her the name of the man at his bank, who would be the executor of his estate. From among the people he hadn't yet looked up, he gave her the name of the one who would be his lawyer from now on. On only two scores did he run into any criticism from her.

He had never carried any insurance—he had considered his merchandise a form of insurance—and now it was too late in life for him to hope to buy a policy at a decent premium. She said she thought a man—not necessarily him, but any man—who didn't carry insurance from the second he got married was seriously inconsiderate.

Then, though apparently she wasn't fazed by the thought of "the inevitable," as she referred to it, she put her hands over her ears when he arranged over the telephone, in a steady, somewhat ironic tone, for his own cremation.

When Aunt Catherine said good-bye to us, she threw her arms around my father as though she would never see him again, and in a frenzied burst of emotion, expressed a sentiment to Ben and me that she'd never voiced before: "Remember, you have a wonderful father. He wants to care for you from his grave...I mean, from...well, just remember that, children."

Ben and I were frantic. "He's *got* to talk to us about it," Ben said. "We've listened to what he had to say long enough."

We cornered him in the library. His satchel was open at his feet and he was looking at an unset diamond he held with pincers. A jeweler's loupe was in his eye.

"This one won't bring as much as the Peddicord, but in some ways, it's more beautiful," he said, dropping his glass into his hand. "However, it'll probably be enough to put you through college, Ben. And there are two more that'll pay your tuition, Lucresse."

"I only want to go to college two years; then I'm going to drama school. I've told you that," Ben said.

"Drama school costs money too, unless you don't have any or you're a genius."

"Maybe I'm a genius." Ben smiled. "What makes you think you're going to die?"

"You *feel* all right," I said firmly.

"Sit down, both of you. Anyone can die. Everyone does." He acted as if this were a comforting fact. "I must make provisions for you in case you're not old enough to make them for yourselves. That's all."

"You *do feel* all right?" I said—this time a question.

My father grew impatient. "Yes, I *feel* all right."

"But I don't *like* your provisions," Ben said. "It may be all right for Lucresse, but I don't want to stay with Aunt Catherine, ever."

"It's not all right for me either," I said.

"There isn't anyone else," my father offered quickly. "She's right. I, and you, suffer from a lack of consideration on my part. I should have thought of this years ago and found someone better suited. But I didn't. I didn't think of myself as dying, the way young people don't. But let's be charitable, to me. Perhaps I'm more of a case of arrested development than lack of consideration."

He seemed so self-satisfied about it that I was angry. "You're not going to die soon; there's no reason you should. And we're not going to Aunt Catherine, ever!" I said.

"I hope you're right." He stuck his glass back up under his eyebrow.

Ben and I left the library. We were nowhere near the right path in our mutual search for escape from impending disaster.

CHAPTER TEN: GAMES

Over the following weeks, Ben, my father, and I wrote a long collective letter to Fred about all of our house help, all of the problems, and all of our longings (at least, that part, I did, even though Ben told me that under *no* circumstances should I tell Fred I missed him so bad that it hurt). Fred wrote back—in a not displeased mood—that he was well, but getting accustomed to feeling tired, and that we should not despair finding suitable help since "you Briards need a bit of getting used to." He also said, in the letter's sole sad passage, that *he* was so used to us that his most arduous task was getting used to life without us.

Every few weeks after that, one of us wrote to him, and Fred's answers indicated that he was indeed gradually adjusting to life without us; he had come to love his sister's flower boxes and his slow, same walk to the village every twilight.

I became fifteen soon after entering Winding Hill High School. I thought of having a party, though it would be retrogressing toward the dim past. So I decided not to. I was being distant with the girls I knew and sacrosanct with the boys—perhaps a delayed reaction to my last date with Arthur. It felt as if I had always been fifteen going on sixteen, but I didn't really look forward to becoming sixteen. It was the future, and I was afraid to expect.

In one week, my father, who had never visited a doctor in my memory, kept voluntary appointments with three—a heart specialist, an ophthalmologist, a dentist. They found his heart, eyes, and teeth in unusually excellent condition for a man of seventy. The teeth man wanted to write up a detailed history of his eating and brushing habits. My father rejected the idea, but his mood of resignation didn't change.

He became selling-happy. The inferior Cellini tray disappeared. The French tapestry came down off the wall for good. A small marble Madonna he'd always cherished vanished from its pedestal.

Ben took to lifting barbells. The Winding Hill gym teacher had decreed that he was too light for the second-string football squad, and Ben was concerned about the possibility of someday being called upon to play a football player. But he was even more concerned and enthusiastic about learning to "throw away" lines, an acting technique of delivering dialogue that was new to him, but a favorite with his new Winding Hill after-school speech teacher.

One afternoon, I was in my room doing homework and wondering if I'd been too inflexibly aloof since moving to Winding Hill—I didn't yet have a best friend and couldn't be counted among the most popular girls who didn't resort to best friends—when my reflection was interrupted by my father calling me, to meet a visitor.

Mrs. Virginia Welch Loder. Soft gray hair that looked blue in the late afternoon sunset shining in the windows from across the river. Narrow oval fingernails. She used her hands gracefully and a lot. Her father had built this house—a house that, we learned, had exchanged owners several times since Mrs. Loder had married and moved away from Winding Hill. Her blue-gray eyes shone when she spoke of her father, her calm voice modulated with pleasure. She was delighted to meet me, hoped that her daughter, Louise, who was a *lovely* girl too, and I would become good friends now that, after her husband's recent death, she and Louise had come home to Winding Hill. They had the little "Hunter" house, and Mrs. Loder smiled at the idea that she, a Welch, was now newer in Winding Hill than we were.

We showed her through the house. Everything about her drew me and made me sorrowful. She knew her way more surely than I. My room had been hers through her child- and girlhood, and her eyes roaming over it made it seem rightly hers still.

Ben came home. The four of us chatted in the living room. Hubert turned on a faucet in the kitchen and embarrassment filled my heart. No doubt the plumbing had been more polite when she'd lived here—her father wanted everything to be so "right" for her and her mother.

My father asked about her husband. Had he posed such a question to Aunt Catherine—even about a husband of a friend of her friend—she wouldn't have spared a detail of retching or muscular ineptitude in a clinical account of his demise. Mrs. Loder barely sighed—it was more an extended exhalation—and said, "We were lucky. He didn't have time to get used to being an invalid. There was one stroke—and then the other."

She then turned the subject to my father. She was glad it wasn't necessary for him to travel to and from the city every day—the wearing routine of so many Winding Hill men. Such a shame. Winding Hill was created to enjoy. If a man saved one disease-ridden tree on his property, wasn't he doing something more worthwhile than he'd do in an average business day in an office? She had to go, but she emphatically told us how glad she was to have come and what a *lovely* time she'd had. She shook hands warmly with all of us, and we all looked warmly understanding.

"She's like a lost little girl," said my father, "who's finally found home, and found she can't go in."

I knew, and hoped, that wasn't the last we'd see of Mrs. Loder.

Making no sense at all, Ben said, "Yes, she's naïve. Not like Felicity."

Felicity. The thought of her filled my heart with lovingness, pushing out all the pity I'd been feeling for Mrs. Loder. Though I hadn't seen Felicity in a long while, she was instantly real—as real as if she were in the room with Ben and my father. Felicity. She might as well have been standing beside me, whispering in my ear. "Caution," she said. Sometimes she made as little sense as Ben. "Caution," I heard again in the place behind my eyes where she had once seen me. Why? No caution was necessary with Felicity. Anybody could tell from half a block away that her hair was an artifice. All her artifices were blatantly apparent, so you knew what was what. "Caution," I heard again. And this time I thought of the pretty blue glints in Mrs. Loder's hair in the sunset. One had to look hard to see that it wasn't real. And Mrs. Loder's gladness about us—did one have to look hard at that, too?

"There's only one thing about her that bothers me," I said. "Everybody she knows is 'lovely.'"

My father's reprimand was immediate. "As I recall, she didn't say that about more than three or four people, and you were one of them, Lucresse."

"But I wouldn't call more than two people I've met in my whole life 'lovely.' That's all."

His voice reverberated the way it did other times in my defense. "Maybe, Lucresse, you don't look for the goodness in people. I have no reason to suspect that Mrs. Loder herself is anything other than lovely. One of the most realistic, sensible, *feeling* people I've met in *my* whole life, which has been a little longer than yours."

"I didn't mean anything against her exactly."

"Then exactly what did you mean?"

"Just that, well, *everybody* can't be lovely. Do you think *I'm* lovely, Ben?"

"No," Ben said, as I was sure he would.

"I don't think so, either, right now," my father huffed. "You have no cause to criticize a woman who's shown us nothing but friendliness. And remember, she's had sorrow, and she's alone."

I wanted to say those were not good enough reasons for me to be convinced she was lovely, but I didn't dare.

Ben tried to placate us both. "I don't see why you're arguing. She's a nice woman. We hardly know her."

But we got to know her better, quite fast it seemed. My father invited her for tea a few days later, and now they were calling each other Virginia and Walter. She couldn't bear the thought of him taking the village taxi to the station and the train to New York when he went. Several times she picked him up and drove him to the station; several times he accepted her offer to drive him all the way to the city, and they spent long days together. She suggested, with her smooth hand on my shoulder, that I call her Ginny. "Thank you," I said, for want of another reply, and held back the "Mrs. Loder."

"And do promise me you'll look up Louise in school," she said.

Louise was in the other junior group and I'd not met her yet.

"Sometimes Louise is a trifle shy about making new friends. She hasn't moved around as much as you. I must get you girls together."

Dutifully, I did seek out Louise Loder the next noon. I asked her homeroom teacher to point her out to me in the cafeteria. She resembled her mother, in height and small features, but her hair was brown and her stance wholly opposite: shoulders held as though to guard her caved-in chest, buttocks shoved under so that the abdomen thrust outward. She was thin, especially thin-legged, but she walked as if she were made of iron from the hips down. She was wearing a tweed skirt, a fussy blouse, ankle socks, and low, dirty sneakers. I expected her voice to be hard to hear. Instead, it was quite loud and little nasal.

"I'm Lucresse Briard," I told her. "Your mother is a friend of my family's."

"You mean Walter Briard?"

"Yes. He's my father."

"She's his friend, all right."

In spite of her rather curt way of accepting my introduction, I felt that she didn't object to me. Her way was just more direct than most girls'. I didn't like or dislike her. Her directness was intriguing.

After school, I saw her coming down the school steps and I walked home with her. We talked about our hair. She wished hers was as long as mine, but her mother said it wouldn't look good. She shrugged and added, "My mother says she and I have the kind of looks that get better as we get older. She wasn't so hot looking either when she was my age. I've seen pictures of her."

"I think your hair is pretty like that."

She shrugged again and laughed. "The truth is, she just believes in short hair. So who am I to argue? She likes to think she's taking care of me."

I wanted her to talk some more, but I didn't want to seem prying. "She does take care of you, doesn't she?"

"I guess so. She bought me this blouse yesterday, just as something extra, because she liked it."

I equated her mother with the several hundred salesladies who had been my clothing advisors, and I envied Louise. The salesladies had wanted me to look attractive for profit; her mother wanted her to look attractive to satisfy her own feelings.

"I used to be very fat," continued Louise, "and I couldn't wear blouses like this. She put me on a diet—I nearly starved to death—and now I'm thin so she gets a big thrill out of buying me stuff like this. I'm still not supposed to eat ice cream and stuff like that."

I couldn't understand why, though I believed she was lucky to have a mother who cared so much about her, I also felt that Louise was unfortunate. I just did. It was a warm, fall afternoon. "Oh, you're skinny enough to eat ice cream now," I said. "Come over to my house and have some with me. I'm sure your mother won't mind. She's coming for tea later."

Her mother was already there, and she embraced us both. Nothing could have made her happier than our meeting. At once I understood what she had meant when she said Louise was sometimes a trifle shy. Around her mother, Louise's voice lost its nasal shrillness; in fact, she hardly spoke. And she smiled more.

When Hubert brought in the tea, my father said he'd changed his mind and would prefer a scotch and soda. "Will you have one with me, Virginia?"

"No, thank you." She looked at him shrewdly. "You know, Walter, I'm afraid you're going to think what I'm going to say is very silly."

"I often think the things you say are silly," said my father good-humoredly. "But you go ahead and say them anyway."

I didn't think Mrs. Loder could look happier than she had when Louise and I had arrived together, but she did now. She broke into a lilting laugh. "Walter, I'm *serious*. What I think is, you need a lift every day about this time. I think you ought to get in the habit of taking a short nap instead."

"Why, Virginia? I'm not tired."

"Some people who are used to feeling energetic don't realize it when they're tired," she explained sweetly. "They think they need some tea or a drink, when actually they need rest."

"All right. You rest. I'll have a drink," said my father, grinning at her.

She laughed again. "What a devilish sense of humor you do have! Remember, you're sixteen years older than I am, I'm delighted to know. I promise you, if you'll start taking a nap every afternoon, I'll do the same in sixteen years. Meanwhile, I'll enjoy my tea." She sipped some. "But do think about it, Walter. Won't you?"

As he took a mouthful of the highball Hubert had just delivered, his face went humorless, as if he were already thinking about it.

I invited Louise to come with me to the kitchen to get some ice cream.

"Darling, do make it a smallish portion," her mother called after us.

I fixed the portions and when Louise surveyed hers, I sensed that she was reluctant to return to the living room with it. "Why don't we go out to the backyard instead?" I suggested, and I shoved open the screen door, which sounded its usual elongated scream.

"What was *that*?" her mother called in alarm.

"Just the screen door," I called back. "We're going outside."

"Oh. Have fun," her mother sang.

We sat on the patio just outside the kitchen. Louise's spoon rat-a-tatted from her plate to her mouth and in seconds, her plate was empty.

"This is the first time I've had this since before my father got sick," she said. "I've lost fifteen pounds since he died—in three months—and only six the three before. He used to sneak me a piece of bread and butter every night."

"I bet you miss him."

"A lot more than the bread and butter. But I sure do miss that too."

Having cut through the woods instead of coming in from Winding Hill Road in front, Ben ambled into the yard and up to the patio. As I explained who Louise was, she retired into her earlier shyness.

Ben could always eat anything, any time of day or night. "I think I'll have some of that," he said, and he swung open the screen door, eliciting the scream.

"What is it, children?" Mrs. Loder caroled.

"It's Ben. Hello." And he disappeared inside to say it more properly. A few minutes later, he returned with a laden plate.

Seeing it, Louise, seemed to lose her shyness as she thrust out her empty one with pleading eyes. "Could I have some more? I'm not usually allowed to have any, I used to be so fat."

"Sure," said Ben, winking. "You're just about right now. Lucresse has always been too skinny."

"So have you," I said.

"Wait till I've had six months with the barbells." He went for the screen door—which once again let loose a shriek.

"Yes?" came Mrs. Loder's voice.

"Just getting..." Ben yelled and he quickly turned on a faucet to muffle the rest of his answer.

Returning with Louise's plate heaped, he said, "Your mother has very good ears."

Louise's manner became direct again, more urgent than on our walk. "And she knows if I had a taste of this, I might ask for more. She puts two and two together fast." Louise devoured the second helping of ice cream as fast as the first. "You know, I like you," she said suddenly, seeming to direct this to both Ben and me. "So I've got to tell you something. My mother didn't tell me this—like I'm going to tell you—right out in the open. But I know it's so."

"What?" said Ben.

"What she wants more than anything, what she's *always* wanted, far back as I can remember— "

"For you to be thin?" I interrupted and Ben silenced me with a look.

"Aside from that." Louise showed no sign that I'd offended her. "She wants this house. She thinks it should be hers."

"You mean because her father had it built?" Ben said. "I can see how she might feel that way."

Louise's lips pressed closed in a firm slit. "She'd do *anything* to get it. And now she thinks she has a chance."

"But my father's not selling it," I said. "At least, he hasn't said anything about selling it yet. It usually takes him a little longer than we've been here, and now he even seems to want to settle down."

"You don't understand," said Louise. "She doesn't want to *buy* it. She doesn't have the money. Otherwise, why do you think she *didn't* and we're in the Hunter dump? She just wants to have it—for nothing."

Ben's eyes narrowed. "And how do you think she hopes to get it—for nothing?"

Louise's eyes went as narrow as Ben's. "It's simple. She hopes to marry your father."

"Gosh!" I said, overcome by the sound of the truth I hadn't surmised.

Louise began to tremble. "If you tell her I said this, I'll swear I didn't, even if you don't like me for it."

"We're not going to tell her," Ben said, almost comfortingly.

Louise stopped shaking.

We went inside. Louise was quiet again, smiling faintly. Ben's manner was easy. Only my own face felt false until Louise and her mother left.

My father observed my odd, blank look. "What *is* the matter with you, Lucresse?"

I bet when Louise looked vapid, her mother didn't ask her about it. Louise must look that way often—and Mrs. Loder didn't know Louise as well as Louise knew Mrs. Loder.

"I was wondering," I began, "did you ever think of marrying?"

"Lucresse!" snapped Ben.

"It's all right," my father said with a chuckle. "Yes, Lucresse, a long time ago. Barbara Stanwyck. A *lovely* girl."

"I don't mean *that*," I said, ignoring his imitation of my imitation of Mrs. Loder's "lovelies." "I mean *really*. Somebody you *knew*. Like Felicity, for instance."

"No, I never thought of marrying Felicity."

The question in the muscles of my lips was, did he ever think of marrying Mrs. Loder, but another look from Ben shut me up. "I was just wondering," I said. "Well, I have to go finish my English assignment."

"What is it this time?" my father asked, so easily dissuaded from the crucial subject.

"I have to write a theme."

"Oh? About what?"

"I don't know. I haven't started it yet. The teacher said we can write about anything interesting. I wish she'd said the Empire State Building or something like that that you could look up stuff about. This way, I can't even get started. I've never been anywhere interesting and don't know anybody interesting and nothing interesting ever happens around here."

I went to my room where I fiddled about for a half hour, putting down my pencil here and there, and forgetting where I put it and having to search for it again. Finally, in bored desperation, I put it to my lined notebook paper and let it go where it would. It wrote a fantastic fairy tale about a beautiful, but conniving lady, who was attempting by all sorts of deceits and ruses to marry a good king who was quite taken with her, in order to do away with him and usurp his kingdom. The only one who knew of her plot was her slave girl, whom she thought she could trust because of the girl's docile nature and dominated devotion. But the slave girl exposed the lady's treachery to the king's loyal courtiers, and they... That was as far as I got; I couldn't think of a way they could rescue their king from his own weakness and foolhardiness.

I told myself it was an addled childish story, not what the teacher meant by something interesting, and I tore it into small pieces. Then I borrowed my father's timetable and wrote nine hundred words about the number of trains that stopped at Winding Hill every day and the variations in their speeds to the city. It included a harsh critique of the confounding nomenclature "local-express." But the fantasy kept haunting me. I wanted to finish it, at least in my mind.

Mrs. Loder was there the following Tuesday, Thursday, and Friday afternoons. She chatted with me while, during part of each visit—after tea, not a highball—my father went upstairs to take a nap. She was the essence of affability.

"Lucresse, you and Louise should see each other more often. You complement each other so."

My translation: "She has a mother and you have a father." Why must one girl have both? Answer: Because she wanted it so, for herself. Secondly, for Louise. Hardly at all, for me.

"I like Louise very much, Mrs. Loder," I said.

"Ginny," she corrected, with a soothing smile.

In my mind, Mrs. Loder remained the Wicked Lady, an image reinforced the day after, when another letter came from Aunt Catherine. It ended, "*...as always, I hope this finds you all in good health. But remember, Walter, in case anything happens, like what I told you when I was there, remember you can always count on me.*"

Ben shuddered and looked fixedly at my father. "You ought to answer her this time, and tell her once and for all, we don't *want* to count on her. Will you, please?"

The fact that my father didn't deny the request outright quickly became more frightening than if he had. What he said was, "I'm going to think about that, Ben. Catherine might not be the best choice to look after you both, after all. Someone nearer—nearer to our way of thinking..."

"You're not still thinking of dying, are you?" I said, feeling a combination shaky and heavy feeling in the pit of my stomach.

"Who is the someone nearer you have in mind?" said Ben, his eyes narrowing perceptibly.

"I'm not at all ready to say," my father said, his jaws obstinate.

"C'mon, Dad," persisted Ben, "you can't make an implication like that and clam up."

"I didn't imply anything. You inferred."

It always upset me and put me at a disadvantage when he resorted to the difference in the meaning of words. It meant my cause was doomed. "All right," I surrendered the point immediately, "both of us inferred. Even though I still think you implied. Who...whom?...who do you have in mind to count on who is nearer?"

"What person?" Ben insisted.

My father handed Aunt Catherine's letter to me and made a helpless gesture. "You answer it, Lucresse. I'm not ready to tell her anything about this yet."

He dropped into his armchair. "You're both right—I did make an implication. But try to understand this. I'm confused. I don't know exactly what I *do* have in mind. I haven't made up my mind. And there are so many things to consider."

"About *what*?" I said.

"About choosing the right person to count on. Is she the right person for all of us? If so, would *she* think she was? Would she be willing to assume such a responsibility? What could I offer in return?" He was rambling, not caring if his dilemma was clear to us.

Ben and I exchanged an anxious glance, and Ben nodded purposefully. *Oh no!* I shook my head to him, but he leveled his eyes at my father and said, "Are you talking about marrying Mrs. Virginia Welch Loder?"

My father's hands collapsed in his lap. His face was nervous, begging. Now he was at the disadvantage, a condition he'd rarely been in in my presence, and it was distressing to witness.

"As I said, there are many things to consider...would *she* consider the idea? I'm not certain she would."

I breathed carefully and didn't talk.

"Haw!" Ben said, reminding me of a Wally Noonan I'd once known.

Instantly, my father's helplessness vanished. Popping upright, he glared angrily at Ben. "And just what do you mean by *that*?"

Ben retreated. "Nothing. Not anything."

How cowardly, I thought. But no worse than I would have done, considering my father's reaction.

Ben recovered, making me retract my mental accusation. "I only meant that I'd bet she *would* marry you."

"You think she cares for me that much?" my father said.

Ben took a deep breath, the kind of breath he'd been practicing with his speech teacher so that his voice could hit the back of a theater, and I knew he was going to speak at this second, as my father would in the same circumstances, no matter what the consequences.

"I don't know how much she cares for you. I just think she wants to marry you. She wants to get back her father's house."

There was a resounding silence. Then my father slowly stood up. "What you said is despicable."

"Unless it's true." Ben held his ground.

"If it's true, then *she's* despicable, and I can't judge anyone."

"We'll see," Ben said. "We'll see."

I didn't know how he meant we would see, but I did know two other things: my father was as angry as I'd ever seen him, and my original theme story—the fairy tale about the lady and the king—still had no ending.

Simultaneously, Ben and I found reasons to attend to other matters. On the upstairs landing, we spoke in whispers. "Ben," I said, "suppose Louise is wrong?"

"Even if she was wrong, she was right. If she wanted to say that about her mother—your 'Ginny'—then her mother probably deserves it."

"I only called her that once or twice."

"I only know one thing. She's not the right one to 'count on' for me, or Dad. I don't know about you."

"Most of the time I don't like her, even though she's nice."

"She's *not* nice," said Ben. "That's what we have to show *him*. It's like Iago and Othello."

Why did he always have to make everything about some play? "It's like Daddy, and her, and us," I corrected. "But you know, sometimes I feel sorry for her. She doesn't know how Louise feels about her."

"That's because Louise is afraid of her right now. But someday..."

"Ben, what'll happen if Daddy marries her?"

"He can't. She doesn't want *him*."

"But he won't be convinced. She wouldn't admit that for anything. She wouldn't admit the truth—she's so *pleasant*."

"Don't worry," said Ben. "I'll get an idea."

A little later, he telephoned Louise and asked her to have a picnic lunch with him the next day, a Saturday. I nudged his elbow, wanting him to say I'd be along, but he brushed me away. Louise asked her mother, who sang out loud enough for me to overhear, "That would be *lovely*." She even offered to supply the lunch. Ben thanked her and told Louise he'd bring a few odds and ends.

The next morning, with Hubert's silent assistance, Ben took a quarter of a baked ham and made four peanut butter and jelly sandwiches. He wrapped them in waxed paper and put them in a paper bag, and, commenting as an afterthought, "Louise might be hungry," he added a bottle of milk and a pint of ice cream.

I didn't see him again until five o'clock. Before he came home, Mrs. Loder called to make sure my father was resting and to say that Louise had had a "lovely time." Ben's cheeks were flushed when he came in and his greeting to my father was perfunctory. Then he called me into his room and closed the door.

Back and forth, back and forth he paced. "We don't have much time," he said intensely. "I saw *her* twice—when I called for Louise and when I took her home. And I'd swear she has ideas now about Louise and *me*. But that doesn't matter. I talked to Louise for two hours. The ice cream helped. She's a nice kid. She's on our side."

"Did she have any ideas?"

"*I* got the ideas—from what she told me."

"What did she tell you?"

"Her mother has it all planned—down to the school she's picked for you and Louise, after she's busy running this house. That'll take all her time, with the repairs she wants to do. So you and Louise are going to boarding school. She hasn't figured out what to do with me yet."

"What!?"

"You heard me. What's more, she's in a hurry. She's already on the lookout for somebody to sublease the Hunter house from her in January. But we'll see about that."

"How, Ben?"

"The less you know about it, the better. You're no good at this sort of thing. I only hope Louise doesn't get scared again."

I asked "about what" several times, but all he would say was, "When the time comes, just don't interfere."

I began to realize "the time" had come the next afternoon when Mrs. Loder arrived for tea. Ben was more than friendly; he was excited by her presence.

She responded in kind, exuding interest in him and his interests. After he had run in and out of the room, bringing his barbells for her to see, she chirped, "Goodness! I never saw a boy with so much energy!"

"He's getting more every year," my father said.

Ben hoisted the barbells to his chest and shouted, "Ginny, you inspire me!" Then, letting the weights drop to the floor with a wall-shaking thump, he sprang over to her and crouched at her feet. "Tell me, Ginny, *why* do you inspire me?"

Her laugh filled the room.

A little satiric, a little self-consciously boyish, Ben said, "Tell me all about yourself, Ginny—what you like, what you *want*. Can't you see, you fascinate me?" He could have been half-joking or all-joking; he was such a good actor you really couldn't tell.

She trilled another laugh, winked at my father, and tousled Ben's hair. "The girls better watch out for you, Ben, you say such pretty things."

"I'm serious, Ginny," Ben continued, his voice almost choking with emotion. "Please, let's talk of serious things."

"All of us?" I said, unable to contain myself.

"We never have—all of us, like this together," Ben reasoned. "Why not?"

"I'll have a scotch and soda," my father said.

"It's time for your nap," said Mrs. Loder.

I wanted to join in. "*What* serious things are you thinking about, Ben? What serious things should we all discuss?"

Giving me a warning look, Ben stood. "I'll get Dad the scotch first," he murmured and hurried to the pantry.

"A dutiful son," my father said.

"And a charmer," Mrs. Loder added while Ben was gone.

Ben returned, handed the drink to my father, then resumed his crouch at Mrs. Loder's feet. "Are you happy...*truly* happy?" he crooned up at her.

"Yes, my dear. I'm happy. Truly," she said softly, perhaps a bit embarrassed.

"*I'm* not," I said suddenly, determined to be included in this play.

"No one asked *you*," Ben said, and then to Mrs. Loder, "But you *could* be *happier*, right?"

"Oh, I don't know."

"There must be something you want," persisted Ben, still in that same crooning tone of great concern. "Everybody wants *something*."

"*I* want you and everybody else to stop telling me when I'm allowed to talk," I volunteered.

"*I* want your father to take his nap," Mrs. Loder said lightly.

"*I* want to know what Ben's point is," my father said between sips of his highball.

"All *I* want is for Ginny to be as happy as *possible*," Ben began, but the doorbell interrupted him. He smiled at Ginny with enormous compassion, then sprinted to answer it. When he returned, it was with Louise and he was talking to her animatedly, bringing her up to date on the "discussion" at hand. Louise smiled nervously and replied to Ben's explanation, "But I don't know anything about my mother's happiness," and she plopped the great weight she no longer carried into a chair.

"Your mother won't answer. Please, *you* tell us, Louise. What would she like above all else?" said Ben.

Louise held her breath for an instant, then she managed, "Oh, a lot of things, I guess."

"Really?" Mrs. Loder was somewhat taken aback.

"Yes," said Louise with conviction. "Really."

"We *could* talk about something else," suggested Mrs. Loder, not nastily.

"I *must* know," insisted Ben of Louise. "What would she like?"

The girl exchanged a glance with her mother that was no less frightening because it was fleeting. Then Louise smiled, her twitches gone.

"I suppose one *must* listen to a child's opinion, now and then," Mrs. Loder said to my father.

I could tell that this remark rubbed him the wrong way. He didn't look at her, and instead addressed Louise. "What *is* your opinion, Louise?"

"I think," began Louise, "well...I think she'd like everything to be the way it was for her before she got messed up with my father and me."

My father rubbed his eyes as though he had difficulty focusing them.

Mrs. Loder nearly shrieked, "Louise! What a thing to say! I've never been 'messed up.'"

"*You* know what I mean," Louise said calmly.

"I *certainly do not!*" rat-a-tat-tatted Mrs. Loder. Then, decrescendoing, "I was married to your father for seventeen years, and I never complained."

"No," Louise said. "You hardly ever talked."

My father started to say something that began, "Virginia, I'm sorry," but she interrupted with an explanation...or defense... "George Loder was not a very talkative man!"

"He talked to *me*," said Louise.

"Louise—my sweet—the way you put it makes what you're saying open to misinterpretation," Mrs. Loder said carefully. "You *know* I didn't spend seventeen years in silence. Didn't I talk to you too? You *know* I did."

"Mostly about how great life used to be when you weren't his wife or my mother—back in Winding Hill, in this house," Louise said in a breathless monotone.

"I don't know what's gotten into you!" Mrs. Loder exploded.

"I don't either." Louise was suddenly puzzled by her own behavior.

"Courage," Ben offered.

"The devil," Mrs. Loder said. "Actually, none of this makes sense. I'm as confused as all of you must be."

We all let that last sentence linger in the air, unanswered, but Mrs. Loder, reddening, couldn't let it die unacknowledged.

"I'm sure you, Ben—and you, Lucresse—would never have maligned your mother like this," she said.

I found my voice. "That was different. She didn't have a chance to tell us how unhappy she was."

"Lucresse, that wasn't necessary," my father said.

"Once and for all, I *wasn't* unhappy. I'm *not* unhappy," Mrs. Loder said.

Louise poked her face forward, self-doubt gone. "And I suppose you don't want this house back more than anything, *oh no*." She spoke with outsized adolescent sarcasm.

Mrs. Loder turned into a tigress. "What are you trying to *do* to me?"

she roared. "I've tried to make *you* happy, Louise. I've even tried to make you *attractive!*"

Ben and I held our breath, controlled witnesses to the mother and daughter finally confronting each other with no control. To tell you the truth, it was exhilarating and we were content—in fact, anxious—to let the scene develop to whatever heights it could reach. But my father's most pressing wish was obviously directly opposed to ours.

"One person's salvation is not necessarily another's," he said gently.

Mrs. Loder's anger shifted to him. "What do you mean, salvation?"

"There's no reward in being attractive to people who aren't attractive to you," he said kindly.

Mrs. Loder shook her shoulders as if to throw off some great burden. "All this nonsense! Happiness and salvation! All anyone can do is get as much as possible out of life, and there are no further rewards." She shot a bitter glance at Louise. "Sometimes I think there are *no* rewards."

Ben's tone was hard and incredulous. "You didn't say a word about making someone else happy, Mrs. Loder."

She turned on him with wrath. "Ben, you are a rotten, nasty boy!"

"'Ruthless' is a better word," my father said quietly.

"Walter, you ought to do something about that boy." Without looking at any of us, Mrs. Loder gathered her purse and gloves.

"Come, Louise," she muttered at the door, and Louise, with an untypical spring in her step, followed her out.

As the house reverberated with the door sounds, my father stared at Ben with a docile, wondering expression.

"Okay, Dad," Ben finally said. "I'm sorry. Do you want me to apologize to her, too?"

"No-o-o," my father said, drawing out the little word. "If you did, I'd have to apologize to you, and I'd hate that."

It was his only admission that Ben had been right, and all he had to say on the subject, except, "Poor Louise...poor Louise." He didn't take a nap and he had two more highballs before dinner.

Mrs. Loder called the next morning to ask if she could drive him to the station, but he said he wasn't going to the city that day, and he didn't invite her to tea.

Ben bounced back to his normal elated, energetic state. "He knows he misjudged her, and that's all we wanted," he told me. "And he's not angry with me."

"No, he's always known you could be ruthless," I said admiringly.

A few days later, Louise and I had a talk in the girls' room in school. "Is she still furious with you?" I asked.

"No. The funniest thing happened. We had a real run-in after we left your house, but since then, she and I are getting along much better. It's like the pressure is off, if you know what I mean. She knows *I* know how she really feels about everything, and she doesn't have to pretend she doesn't. How's your father?"

I was thinking so hard about how nice it must be to be ruthless if you felt ruthless, or to have somebody else know how you really felt, or to know yourself the truth of how you felt that I almost didn't hear the question. "Oh, my father? He's the same as ever," I said comfortably. "When you're his age, you don't change much."

CHAPTER ELEVEN: THE STRATEGISTS

The removal of Mrs. Loder from our lives—oh, my father saw her now and then, but not as frequently as he began to see other people—imbued us with fresh vitality. Without being aware of it, I smiled more. Boys in my class invited me to football games and parties, and once in a while the movies on Saturday night. The nearest theater didn't sport a midnight show, and I was satisfied to be seen often enough among the girls who were partnered.

With my first date, I was curious, slightly on guard. But after a few experiences, smiling in a conspiratorial, comradely way at the other escorted girls, I learned how to handle the customary good-night kiss, affectionately if not passionately. I bought more clothes and Ben and my father came to accept the facts of my more active social life.

At almost seventeen, I was confident enough to choose the boys I would kiss with more discrimination. Ben, ready to be graduated from high school, had promoted himself from the lead roles in school plays to bit parts in the county's Little Theatre productions. My father didn't talk of dying anymore. He was again buying nearly as much as he was selling; newly purchased antique vases and a collection of water colors helped restore our living room's cluttered appearance, despite Hubert's best efforts. Hubert had spoken perhaps twenty sentences more during the previous year than he had the year before. We were living in what none of us recognized as a hiatus between stirring events.

The first one to develop started after the first performance of the Little Theatre's rendition of *Liliom*, Ferenc Molnár's classic drama about a wife-beater whose wife so adores him that she claims at the end of the play that "someone may beat you and beat you and beat you—and not hurt you at all." Ben played the Second Policeman with a particularly rich, menacing air. The dressing room shared by the male supporting members of the cast was crowded with actors and visitors. Still, one couldn't help noticing Lois Carrington when she came in.

From the back or three-quarter view, she looked about eighteen, the young, country-eighteen of popular fiction. She had a small, rounded figure with firm upper arms and a straight neck. Yet it was her pinafore dress and braided reddish-brown hair that helped mostly to create the eighteen impression. When she turned about full face, you realized from the tiny hollows in her cheeks and under her eyes that she was nearer forty.

I was there to tell Ben that my father and I had enjoyed the show, that we had a ride home, and that if he didn't want to come with us, he could walk. But it was hard to deliver the message. Lois Carrington was hard to interrupt and she was saying, of the father of three who was playing Liliom, "In all honesty, I do think Carl could be more bitter, more biting, in the third scene. Don't you think so, Ben?"

Ben was removing his makeup. He prefaced his answer with a wry, superior smile. "I'd play the whole thing differently."

"I *know* you would. I just *knew* it. I've been watching you at rehearsals, Ben, and I must say, I've thought all along, you're the only one who's really *in* the play, if you know what I mean."

"Yeah."

I butted in. "Ben?"

"Oh, Lucresse...how did Dad like it? This is my sister. Lois Carrington, actress and treasurer extraordinaire."

"Hello. Daddy liked it fine. So did I. It was all right."

"So you're Ben's *sister!* Ben, you didn't tell me you had a *sister!*"

"Daddy wants to know if you're coming home with us, or walking," I said, ignoring her.

"Ben, you're not going right *now*, are you? I have my car," said Lois.

Ben didn't even look at me. "Tell Dad I'll be along later. And here. Take these socks with you. And wash them, will you? They're the only black ones I have."

"I'll leave them on your dresser for *you* to wash," I replied. And I about-faced.

My father and I played gin rummy until Ben got home—after two o'clock.

"Did I seem tough enough to you? Did I convince you?" Ben asked my father immediately.

"Yes, you convinced me," my father said. "Who is Lois Carrington?"

Ben lifted his eyes, and his guard, at me. "She's the treasurer of the company. She could have been a fine actress if she hadn't married the man she did."

"Carrington...Carrington..." my father mused. "I think I know him. I rode into New York with him on the train a couple of times. Has his own accounting firm, a man about my age."

"I don't know her husband," Ben said shortly.

"He let me know he had a very young wife." My father was unquelled. "Seemed the fact was his special pride."

"Since you're both so interested, she's thirty-three or thereabouts," Ben said.

"Or thereabouts," I said.

"I didn't see old Carrington there tonight," my father said blithely.

"He never goes anywhere she goes, not that that's any of *our* business," Ben said.

"See that you don't make it your business," my father said.

"All I'm interested in is the role I'm playing." Ben's mouth was wrathful.

"Rather, that's what you're *most* interested in," my father returned.

"I'm glad you enjoyed the performance so much you couldn't stop talking about it," Ben said bitterly.

My father met Lois the very next morning. Crisp, with a Peter Pan collared blouse and a dirndl skirt, she dropped in to give Ben what she called with a merry, little-girl laugh, "a small present of something every man should have more than one pair of." The package contained three pairs of black socks.

Her attention then turned to me. "Are you going into the theater too, Lucresse? It was my first love."

Many years later, I learned something relatives of famous people know, unless they're asses: how to distinguish between people who are interested in them because their relatives are famous, and sincere people. But this was my first round with someone who wanted to know me because I was Ben's sister, and Ben was not yet famous. I was suspicious, but not wholly antagonistic.

"No, I don't like to act." I oddly felt as if I were lying.

"How odd," she might have commented, from her expression, but my father didn't leave her the opportunity.

"I think I'm acquainted with your husband. He's an accountant, isn't he?"

"Yes," she said.

"A nice man. A very nice man."

She mouthed a cordial, flattered smile. "That's what most people say when they mean the fatherly type."

Pure hatred flitted across my father's face. Ben didn't appear to notice. My father forced it away and asked, "So, you're fascinated with acting?"

"Yes, indeed!"

"You and Ben have a good deal in common then. Tell me, what roles have you played?"

"Where?"

"Anywhere. Here at Winding Hill."

"Well, actually, I haven't played any here—yet. There haven't been any roles that suited me."

"I see," my father said.

"She's played Desdemona in summer stock," Ben said.

"I see."

"I have a good idea, Ben," she said abruptly. "Let's have lunch and read *Othello* this afternoon."

We didn't see much of Ben for the rest of the weekend. Once, when Lois honked for him Sunday, three hours before curtain time, my father asked, "Do you and Mr. and Mrs. Carrington eat all your meals together, Ben?"

"He's out of town, didn't I tell you?" said Ben, dashing out.

"Do you think he's in love with her?" I asked after the walls stopped vibrating from the door slam.

"He's in love with himself," murmured my father, "and she flatters him."

"That's what I think too." I hadn't actually thought any such thought before. "It's not like it was with Felicity."

"No, that was healthy, compared to this."

"Poor *Mr.* Carrington. I think you ought to make Ben leave her alone," I said righteously.

"I've thought of Mr. Carrington. Though no doubt he's aware of all the Bens there must have been. But whose advice has the power of a boy's ego?"

Of course I had no answer.

My father's displeasure with Ben pleased me. Somehow it repaired my wounded self-esteem from a lifetime of failed attempts to be noticed for who I truly was—though my identity still mostly eluded me. If Ben was bad, somehow I was good. Also, it seemed to me that Ben didn't treat me with sufficient respect unless we were mutually embroiled in some crisis, such as the one with Mrs. Loder, and he had been particularly distant and disrespectful since he'd taken up with Lois Carrington.

"Don't try to give him advice," I said. "Lay down the law to him."

"*My* law?" my father said, incredulous. "The law of society? Right now, that's not *Ben's* law. He will obey only his own law. And so will she." His eyes suddenly narrowed, seeing a light that was invisible to me in the darkness of the situation. "And so will *she*."

"But she's..." I couldn't think of an acceptable synonym for a woman who was promoting an affair with a boy half her age while she was married to a proud man twice her years. I couldn't think of the name for that kind of conscious manipulation and deceit.

My father supplied what I considered a mistaken euphemism indeed.

"She's a coward." Nevertheless, in view of his disapproval, during the next week, he showed uncharacteristic patience as Ben charged away time after time at the sound of Lois's horn. We watched her slide over to let Ben slide into the driver's seat. She always tapped a quick little kiss on his cheek as he started up the car. My father never asked Ben where or with whom he was going, didn't wait up for him after any of the five *Liliom* performances.

My patience was at a breaking point. And it burst completely the following Saturday morning when Ben, having arisen late, ambled yawning into the living room where my father was still ruminating about whether to hang the watercolors or not. His remarks made me wonder if he'd gone out of his mind.

He started innocently enough. Ben had mentioned trying to find a summer theater job. "Are you still interested?" my father asked.

"Sure," Ben said.

"All of the summer theater offices are in the city."

"I know that."

"How do you intend to get there and back, 'making the rounds,' as they say?"

Ben moved the watercolor he was fingering a quarter of an inch. "I can take the train, but I can also get a ride."

"Every day? It may take you a few weeks of looking."

"Most every day."

"With whom?" said my father, as if he really didn't know.

Ben distractedly inspected the watercolor picture. "Lois has a car."

My father jutted the one he was holding closer to his face. "Seems to me this is a good time to get you a car of your own."

Ben took him up on the idea instantly, without a pause for thanks or elaboration. He called Lois, and she went with him and my father to a dealer's showroom that very afternoon. Because Ben insisted, I waited at home—consumed by unspeakable rage.

I thought if you told the truth—if you could just figure out what that was—you would win! Louise had told the truth to Mrs. Loder and now they had a good relationship. Ben had been ruthless, and my father had appreciated and respected him for it. But now Ben was sneaking around with a married woman. I had ruthlessly suggested that my father lay down the law and stop it, and instead he was rewarding Ben with a car?! This made no sense at all.

All three—Ben, Lois, and my father—soon returned in a snazzy, red convertible, and Lois kept touching Ben's hand that jingled with the keys and saying she thought it was "just too perfect."

That afternoon, Ben drove Lois to the state park where they planned to study *Hamlet*, and he didn't return until after my father and I had gone to bed. My father was probably instantly asleep, but I lay awake until one thirty—waiting, listening, wondering how Ben could act any way he pleased and still end up on top—and when I finally drifted off, he still wasn't home.

Out of a generous impulse that he could scarcely avoid, though it was sustained longer than I anticipated—for the entire last week of school—Ben drove me to school every morning. We had almost nothing to say to each other, as though we'd never known each other very well. After school, he and his car vanished before I could get to the parking area. He, and it, and Lois were together every afternoon, most dinnertimes, and during every evening until the morning hours began.

The day after Ben graduated—a ceremony my father and I attended, but tactfully, Lois did not, and in which Ben had shallow interest—I decided I must demand an explanation from my father for rewarding Ben's behavior with a car. I didn't expect him to take it away, only to admit that it was a grave error.

After trying to stay awake so late on many nights waiting for Ben, I myself slept quite late the morning after Ben's graduation. And when I got up, I was forced to weigh the intelligence of talking seriously to anyone in our household, when I was accosted by three voices coming from separate locations throughout the house, all ranting from separate worlds.

"The play's the thing," boomed Ben from his room, "wherein I'll catch the conscience of the king."

"Who *told* him to put them away?" my father was saying in an attacking tone, contrapuntal to the bang of doors and the scrape of furniture in the living room. "The man can't keep his hands off anything in sight!"

"He says there were fourteen," came Hubert from downstairs, his ordinarily hushed voice at a wild, high pitch. "I put away only ten! If there are just three lying around, it is not my fault. I *told* him they'd go lost if they weren't hung or put away!"

The sound of Hubert speaking that way magnetized even Ben away from his royal role, and he and I sped to the living room to get an explanation from my father. But the sight of us supplied my father with a target for his attack. "Did *you* take one of the watercolors?" he accused both of us.

"No!" I said.

"I wouldn't want one of them," Ben said. "You don't have to yell at *me*."

"I don't have a chance to *talk* to you lately," my father said angrily.

"Not since the convertible!" I snapped, my sleepiness transformed by self-righteous rage.

My father ignored me. "One of the watercolors has disappeared."

"Maybe..." I began, hoping to think of a question that wouldn't compound his anger, but would instead instantly make him respect my ruthless truth-telling about Ben and that stupid car.

But any reaction was deflected by Hubert's meek entrance carrying the rolled-up missing painting. "It was in the hall closet. *I* didn't put it there, Mr. Briard. *You* were going to take this one to New York—do you remember, sir?"

My father took the roll from him, saying, "There's been too damn much hiding things around here," and he waved Hubert away.

"*I* haven't been hiding anything," I said piously.

"I want to go over a couple of speeches before I pick up Lois," Ben said, all open and above board, scowling at me. He was so intent on putting me in the place he wanted me to keep, the empty space out of his affairs, that my father's next remark caught him off guard.

"You've accepted her hospitality so often recently, why don't you invite her over here to dinner tonight?"

"I don't know..." Ben said.

"Is Mr. Carrington back?" my father asked, as if it made no difference to him whether the answer was yes or no.

"No, but..."

"Then I insist. Hubert's not too put out to fix a decent meal."

Ben didn't argue. He left without going over the Shakespeare again.

My father wouldn't explain this latest move to me; he just looked aggravatingly secretive and happy when I asked about it, and I had to wait—again—for dinnertime.

When Lois arrived, my father seemed excessively glad to see her. Like a fond uncle, he took both her hands in his, saying with old-world civility, "Welcome, my dear." He called her "my dear" frequently, an address he'd never applied to me. Before dinner, he offered her a drink, and to my and Ben's sharp surprise, he offered Ben one too. But to all appearances, no one was more important than Lois Carrington. My father's attentiveness, and the drink, kept her talking.

By the time Hubert served dinner, she'd become a little loose-moving. I noticed that she dropped a mouthful of potatoes off her fork as she said, "Mr. Briard, if my father had been anything like you, I wouldn't have..." and stopped.

"Wouldn't have what, my dear?" said my father kindly.

"Can I be dreadfully frank?" She dropped her fork in the mound of mashed potatoes.

"Of course," he said with enormous sympathy.

"If my father had been like you, I wouldn't have married Leland Carrington."

"You wanted a father, so to speak? Someone to take care of you?" my father responded, with great interest and compassion.

"You're so understanding."

I stole a curious glance at Ben. He avoided it.

"But surely you know, my dear, few mistakes are irrevocable?" my father said.

Ben's eyes rose slowly. We all stared at my father, who, I knew from experience, was plunging into one of his philosophical moods.

"You're still a very young woman," he continued. "Certainly you will rectify this error soon?"

The shadow of deep feeling vanished from Lois's face. Her eyes on my father were clear and curious.

"There are no rules about *when* one must find happiness," he went on. "I, for example, didn't meet my wife until we were both a number of years older than you."

Lois shook her head hopelessly, indicating that she considered his past so far removed from her own present that there was no possibility of comparison.

"Don't close your mind, my dear, out of misplaced kindness. Look at it this way—what a lucky accident it was that you and Ben met when you did."

"What?" Ben said, and his lips didn't close immediately after pronouncing the *T*.

"It seems apparent that Ben has the assets you want and need," my father continued. "In spite of his years, he's mature. I'm sure he'll take care of you..."

"What?" Ben repeated, shifting in his chair.

My father's words came faster. "It goes without saying, he won't be able to provide many of the material advantages for a while. However, after he finds a place for himself in the theater, which shouldn't take *too* many years after he's had adequate training—and during that time you could be carving a niche for *yourself*, as an actress, something you've always wished to do..."

"Dad!" Ben said.

Lois's face stiffened. "Mr. Briard," she said coolly, "you've rushed to conclusions." Gathering her thoughts rapidly, she softened her face. "I couldn't leave Mr. Carrington."

My father looked to Ben.

"Of course not," Ben said.

"Oh. It was I who made the mistake."

"Ben has a car now," I said, hoping to revive the conversation. They all glared at me.

"It's only that I *assumed*," my father said with deep embarrassment. "I hope you don't think I was trying to order your lives."

"Not at all, Mr. Briard," Lois said, sending a twinkling smile to Ben. "We can't always have what we want."

Ben didn't smile back. My father compensated for that with a grin that was abnormally intense. "Not always," he said. "Still, we usually want what we *have*."

Ben took Lois home early, and for once returned immediately after dropping her off. When he came in, he couldn't contain himself. "Dad, you might have gotten me into a lot of trouble," he exploded. "*I* didn't want to *marry* her."

"What *did* you want, Ben?" asked my father.

"I don't know..."

All three of us knew this truth. It was naked and unconfused.

Ben jumped to surer ground. "The point is now you've ruined everything. You scared her half to death."

"Any alliance that doesn't have a future is automatically at its end," my father said soberly.

Ben nodded. "You say the most obvious things and make them sound important."

My father didn't attempt to conceal how pleased he was with himself.

"I get to keep the car, don't I?"

"Certainly," my father said. "It's only a small part of what you really want." His sense of winning and well-being exploded in a hearty laugh. "And we *all* know what that is!"

"I don't see what's so funny about it."

My father laughed till he roared. Without intending to, I laughed too. Last of all, Ben started. The truth was so obvious, so ruthless, so funny that it reinfected all of us and we in turn reinfected each other, and none of us could stop laughing for a long, long time.

CHAPTER TWELVE: LEAVINGS

Once again, life was normal, and once again, after a couple of months, I had the feeling that nothing interesting ever happened. It was at the height of this mood, in the middle of the summer, that Aunt Catherine's monthly, but this time unique, letter arrived. In it, she invited us all to visit her house in Sapulpa.

The immediate collective reaction to the invitation was intense surprise; she had not issued such an invitation before, and a visit from her to *us* was long overdue. My father's and Ben's reactions were undiluted with not so much as a drop of acceptance. Two semi-major parts were in the offing for Ben before he was to leave for college in the fall. And my father didn't consider going for a moment.

"Of course I'm better off here," he said. "But, Lucresse, it might do you, and Catherine, a lot of good if *you* went for a couple of weeks."

"How?" I asked, unwilling right off to admit that my reaction was more open to persuasion than theirs.

"You've never spent a night away from home," said my father. "And Catherine can feel she's reciprocating for all her visits to us."

"But what would I *do* there?"

"If I know Catherine, she'll find enough for you to do."

While making it clear that I protested, I let myself be talked into it rather easily. Winding Hill was comfortable, but it had long since lost the charm as well as the anxiety of a new place. I had been wondering for a long time what Aunt Catherine's home was like and what she was like in it.

"Don't you want to come, too?" I entreated Ben. "Aren't you curious?"

He said he was, but he was more curious about whether or not he'd get one or both roles he'd tried out for.

Though I could imagine Sapulpa, I'd never been there. And going meant I could tell my friends about the contemplated trip in bored, yet glowing, terms. Those who were also contemplating trips this summer weren't going to go alone—like I was—and the fact that they would be vacationing in cooler spots than Winding Hill and I was going to a hotter one didn't affect their envy of, or my pride in, my independence. The largest triumph was when Ben almost changed his mind about going after my father bought my plane ticket for my first flight.

Considering the extravagance of my expectations, the flying experience was bound to be a disappointment. Except for the take-off and the landings en route, the sense of vibrating stillness in air that all land animals experience was plain dull.

But my excitement was renewed when Aunt Catherine, meeting me at the Tulsa airport with her husband, Joe, kept saying, "Are you all right, Lucresse? She's all right, Joe." Joe repetitively bobbed his thrilled, mute face. He took my bag, and driving to Sapulpa, recovered his voice, saying an agreeable, "Uh-huh, sure thing," every little while all the way.

Sapulpa was as flat as Winding Hill was curved, and more blistering hot than Chicago had been in my one summer's stay there. But neither Sapulpa nor Aunt Catherine had anything to do with the fact that Sapulpa is where I started my way to what might have been—to this day, I really couldn't tell you for sure—madness.

Aunt Catherine's little house, like all the others on the block, had the curtains drawn against the burning sun. Inside, it was dark and stifling.

"This time of day everybody smart's takin' a tepid bath," Aunt Catherine informed me. "But theys'll be along here later to meet you. I told 'em, after supper."

"Yeah, uh-huh," echoed Joe. "We all sure heard about you and yours for a long time from her here."

"Now do you have to go say everything you ever heard?" Aunt Catherine affectionately reprimanded him.

The ten or twelve people who came over, fanning themselves, had two things in common: they all were Aunt Catherine's age or older, and they all remembered her sister, Jen. "Poor Jen," they echoed Aunt Catherine's reference to her, and the Jen that appeared to me out of their minds was a girl not much older than me. Only one of Aunt Catherine's friends, a scrawny, old lady with a frizz of white curls and a perpetual, secretive smile, a Mrs. Dunhamly, speculated as to the Jen of later years who had become my mother.

She gave my arm a startlingly tight squeeze and hissed at me through a wheezing laugh, "Don't you make no mistake about it, girl—from all their sadness and sighs. That Jen was a right happy Miss. She done just as she pleased, and they aren't as sorry about her as they let on. They just feel they gotta act sorry about anybody that's died, 'cause they're so scared of bein' dead." She coughed a giggle.

I glanced around at the other people talking to each other, and back at Mrs. Dunhamly. She was older than all of them. I thought of how old Fred was...and the night he almost died...and how the shock of it obliterated everything else that had happened that night all because of me acting any way I pleased—to the point where the box of time that it all fit in no longer *was*, which meant *it* no longer was, which is why I'd never spoken of it.

"But death is a sad thing," I said.

"To who?" she came back at me, bright and challenging.

"To...everybody, I guess."

"No t'snot," she rebutted. "Most folk, like them here, act like they do 'cause they imagine it's sad for the dying. It may be sad, some of the times, for *them* that's left *living*, but sure t'isn't sad for them that die. Them living are thinkin' a lie, a plain lie. Though maybe I'm the only one that knows so."

She leaned her wrinkly face closer to me. "I *know*. Y'see, I died once-t."

"You *did?*!"

"Ten years ago," she said matter-of-factly. "One minute my nephew and his silly wife was running around like their heads got cut off, and then I went. The doctor even signed the medical paper. When I come to, they was havin' the time of their lives grievin'—you know, so happy it wasn't them."

She sucked in her breath, holding it in gulps, making her laughter almost soundless. "Girl, you shoulda seen their faces! Right away, they wants to know what it was like. I told them, like nothing, plain, old nothing. Like a piece of ice melts in the sun. But do you think they believe me? No siree."

She cackled again. "Everybody just wants to go on bein' scared of something they don't know for sure about. It makes them feel more important that way."

"You think so?" I said uncomfortably.

"Sure thing. Why else they go on about heaven and hell, and put on funeral parties—the bigger the better?"

I was giving that thought my most perplexed attention when Aunt Catherine poked her taut, kindly face between us. She moved me into a conversation with a fat woman who kept rearranging her dress over her thick thighs, and she didn't let me near Mrs. Dunhamly again until the visitors were leaving, en masse.

"I hope to see you again," I said politely to all as they departed.

"Mine's the fourth house to the left, with the dead tree in the front," Mrs. Dunhamly said with a wink. "Come see me any old time."

"Poor, old soul," Aunt Catherine sighed as they went out the door. "She's harmless, but a real embarrassment."

"Uh-huh," said Joe. "She always talks like that."

"You mean something is wrong with her?" I asked.

"Well, not enough to be carted off to Vinita, I don't guess," said Aunt Catherine. "Though sometimes I do wonder. She harps on death all the time, and in such a way! Thinks she knows all there is to know about it 'cause she claims she was dead once. And everybody knows, *nobody* knows about *that*."

Joe's meek face was unresentful, but puzzled. "She's always going to funerals, and acting like they was celebrations. She goes to *everybody's*, whether she knew the body or not. Didn't she go far as Pawhuska one time if I remember rightly, Catherine?"

"That's enough of Mrs. Dunhamly," she cut him short. "She's just one of those addled souls nice people have to put up with."

In the next few days, Aunt Catherine kept me busy with the daughters and nieces and sons and nephews and neighbors of the guests who had been over, and Mrs. Dunhamly, not having a young representative, was dismissed. I made mental notes of the differences between my Winding Hill friends and these boys and girls. Those at home, and I—I shamefully had to admit to myself—appeared younger than this collection. In our own minds, we were to remain "kids" until some distant, hardly realized date when we would be released from the final confines of youth—college. Here, though some of the boys were planning to spend time in further education—to become petroleum engineers seemed the most prevalent reason—the girls were already seeing themselves as child-bearing wives. Where my girlfriends' and my interest in sex was still wondering, theirs seemed built on quiet knowledge. I found the girls' talk over lunch dull, but at the same time, I got the feeling that I didn't know much about my world and they knew everything about theirs, and that nothing I was sure about was very important...or even true.

Each time I came back to Aunt Catherine after a session of socializing, she asked if I'd had a good time, and I quickly developed the ability to assume a convincing smile and tell her what she wanted to hear. On my fourth day's return, my conditioned reaction smile was unwarranted. Aunt Catherinc greeted me making sorrowful pigeon noises in her throat.

"You're to call Ben," she said.

"Ben?"

"Long distance. Oh, Lucresse. Right away, you poor child. I wrote down the number of the right operator."

I didn't dare ask her more.

I had rarely spoken to Ben on the telephone. His voice was different—deeper, older. He didn't wait for me to say more than hello.

"Lucresse, it's best for you to come home. Felicity is going to fly to Tulsa and meet you, tomorrow. She'll come back with you..."

"Ben... Ben? What's the matter?"

"It's all over," he said slowly. "This morning...Daddy was fine..."

It was a long time since he had called my father Daddy.

"...he and I, and Hubert, were lifting off the marble table top...he was going to have it crated for somebody. It was too heavy...too heavy, I guess...I didn't know it was too heavy..." Ben became fainter, a sing-song monotone.

"Ben, what happened?"

"He's dead, Lucresse."

Coming and receding, from a longer distance than there was between us, I heard him say again, "It's all over. He told me who to call... the men in New York, and Felicity, and you, of course."

Aunt Catherine was urging a chair under me. I kicked it back. "Ben, I don't believe you."

"Yes, you do," he said without the least argumentativeness. "Stay with Aunt Catherine until she takes you to meet Felicity tomorrow. We'll talk more tomorrow night."

"Ben, it's impossible."

"I'll see you tomorrow night. I know how you feel."

"I don't feel."

When I hung up, Aunt Catherine was clutching the chair I'd refused, her head bent over its back, tears falling in rhythmic drops onto her hands. I wanted to say something to relieve her agony. What came out was, "Don't, please don't."

"Oh, Lucresse!" she said through a heaving sob, "I'm so sorry—so real and truly sorry!"

"Don't," I said again, and went to a curtained window. "Do you mind if I pull this aside?" I said, yanking the flowered material into a tight cluster of pleats. "I never looked out here."

She collapsed into the chair, floral patterned too, and rubbed her face into a handkerchief. Her voice was muffled. "You poor, poor child. First Jen...now this."

I stared out at the wavering heat waves on the road. I wondered if the asphalt was really hot enough to fry an egg on. I didn't want to look at Aunt Catherine. Nothing she was saying made any sense, and I was helpless to hush her.

"I've got to pack," I said. "I'm going home tomorrow."

"I know. I know," she wept. "I offered to go with you, Lucresse. I want you to know that." She stopped crying. "I told Ben...but he said no, the arrangements was made. I don't understand...from what Walter told *me*...oh, Lucresse, I *am* sorry."

She followed me into the bedroom I'd been using. I packed fast. I was anxious to get home. Everything would be all right, if I were home. "I hope the flight back is fast," I said.

In the middle of folding a sweater, and visualizing myself putting it into my drawer at home, it occurred to me that home wouldn't be the same. Winding Hill wouldn't be the same. Nothing in the world would be the same—if the insane words Ben had said were true. I dropped the sweater any which way into the suitcase and turned to Aunt Catherine. "Where's Joe?" I asked.

"Why...at the store. Oh, Lucresse, forgive him. I called him, and he should of come straight home, but I told him you weren't here. I didn't expect you for another while."

"I hope he comes soon," I said. "I hate to leave you alone, the way you're feeling."

She stared at me as though I'd said it was a freezing day. "But, Lucresse, you're not going until tomorrow. Joe and I will take you to meet that woman. *Tomorrow*, dear."

"I'm going to see Mrs. Dunhamly now."

"Lucresse, no! Not that crazy old woman, at a time like *this?*"

"Yes." I remembered the directions clearly, the fourth house to the left with the dead tree in front. I hoped the old woman would be home. I closed the suitcase and started out of the room.

"I'll go with you!" Aunt Catherine nearly shrieked, chasing after me. "Have a cup of tea first! Or a Dr Pepper, if you like! I'll fix you something to eat. You need nourishment..."

"I'm going now, Catherine. Alone."

Mrs. Dunhamly's front room was bare and as bereft looking as the leaning tree trunk outside it. It was smaller and hotter than any room I'd ever been in, but Mrs. Dunhamly's welcome was heartier than any I'd ever received. My very presence made her tingle with giggly excitement. And I didn't feel required to tingle back.

"Tell me more about what you were telling me the other night," I said immediately.

"You was one of the few that showed sense enough to listen," she said happily. "I *hoped* you'd come see me while you was hereabouts."

"My brother, Ben, called me on the telephone today. He said our father died. I know I should believe him. I know he wouldn't say that unless it was true. But I still don't believe him. And I know it's so. I'm going home tomorrow because it's so. I want you to explain that."

"You'll believe it when you can carry on at the funeral," she said. "That's what they're for. To make folks believe what they're too scared to believe."

In a mental, reasonable, detached way, I told her, "But he didn't want a funeral. He wanted to be cremated, immediately. It probably has already been done, knowing my father and Ben."

"It don't make no difference, once you understand that death isn't anything. Nothing a-tall."

"It means he won't be there anymore. Not even...his body."

That was hard to say. I couldn't think of my father's body; I could only think of him, the person with a body, alive.

"Long as you don't get trapped thinkin' he's gone here or there, to heaven or t'other place, you don't need no funeral. It don't make no difference," said Mrs. Dunhamly.

"I'm to think, he's just...gone? Where?"

"Just gone. To no place. And since you know that, it's not *that* much different than if he was *here*. See?"

"No."

"He's *no* place, child. He just *ain't*."

I kept quiet. She sniffed, hesitating, the first smattering of sympathy she indicated. "Since he's no place *else*, you could talk to him if you want. Now don't *you* go look on me like I was ready for Vinita—that's where we keep the crazy folk of Oklahoma—I'll tell you something I haven't told the others. Knowing what I do, I talk to the Colonel—that's my husband—all the time. Whenever I feel like it."

She giggled. "Prob'ly I talk to *him* more than I talk to the folks still around here. I'll tell you another thing, girl. Sapulpa ain't no big town like Kansas City where you can pick and choose the folks you want to know. Here, a sensible soul has a hard time finding another to talk to."

For a long time I'd suspected that Aunt Catherine, for one, wasn't as sensible as she claimed to be. Now, with my mind awakened to new thoughts by this unusual woman, I was sure she wasn't sensible and I was ready to dismiss her. At the same time, while I was persuaded of the old woman's sense, I wasn't sure I could make it my own. "I don't know if I could talk to my father," I said.

"Do what you like, but I can tell you, it's worth a try."

I left, stunned with hope and anticipation. I might say anything I wished to my father, even things I wouldn't say if he were beside me. I didn't feel the heat of the air or the sidewalk I walked on. I didn't see Aunt Catherine's next-door neighbor standing with a hose at the edge of his neat, little lawn, watering a young tree across the walk on the patch of grass extending to the curb. He may have assumed I would pause, to allow him to redirect his hose, or he may have been, for reasons of his own, in as dense a daze as mine. Whatever the case, he didn't redirect his spray and I didn't miss a step. We met at the inevitable second and I was soaking wet from shoulders to knees.

"I'm sorry...I'm so sorry...I certainly am sorry," the neighbor man said.

What was he so sorry about? floated in my brain as I walked on. Was it what Ben had said and what Aunt Catherine had also said she was sorry about? Or was it the comparatively inconsequential fact that this man had gotten me wet?

"That's all right," I said over my shoulder.

I explained my wet clothes to Aunt Catherine.

"But I don't see how come you didn't *see...*" she began. "Never mind.

Even in this weather, a person could still catch their death, sopping like that. Better change."

I went to the room where my suitcase was, closed the door, removed my sticky blouse and skirt, and lay down on the bed, ready to pursue my newfound rites. At first I was snared in self-conscious silence, embarrassed by the first words that came to mind. I auditioned them twice, mouthed them without a voice. Then I whispered them. "Daddy, do you think I'm sexy enough for college next year?"

I shivered in the strange, stifling room. I heard him answer, "Of course I think so. Didn't I tell you you'd be a beautiful woman?"

"You *really* think so?" I said aloud.

"Of course," came the answer, as clear as only a voice in the mind can sound.

"Lucresse?" Aunt Catherine inquired from the other side of the door. "Did you get out of those wet things?"

I didn't answer, paralyzed momentarily by her rude interruption.

"Lucresse? Did you change?"

There seemed only one answer, one of high drama, that she would never know the true meaning of. "Yes," I called vigorously, "I changed. I sure have."

I dressed and, claiming to need a breath of sizzling air, went out and stretched out on the grass as far back in the small backyard as I could get. I told my father about Mrs. Dunhamly and paused, thinking again of all that she'd said. It seemed to me that the world really belonged more to the dead than the living, by virtue of their majority. Death wasn't the least frightening. It was nothing a-tall. All the people who'd ever lived had died; all who ever would live, would, too. I told my father I wouldn't have thought of any of this if it hadn't been for Mrs. Dunhamly, and that he and I may never have gotten together again, like this. He said we would always be together.

I came back into the house humming the thumping melody of my high-school song, whose words I'd already forgotten... "Al-ways to-geth-er, in bad or fair weath-er..."

Aunt Catherine shook her head at me wonderingly. "It's wonderful to see you so cheerful, Lucresse—in spite of everything. I was afraid that poor, old soul would depress you."

"She's the most cheerful person I ever met."

"You got to remember, she's a little off."

"Maybe not as much as a lot of other people."

Aunt Catherine arranged for a special service at her church for eight p.m. I couldn't consider thinking about, much less talking to, my father there, in the presence of her well-meaning friends. I refused to go. She and Joe reluctantly left me alone for an hour—time I spent telling my father that I didn't feel desolate.

I don't think Aunt Catherine recognized the woman at the airline's desk the next morning as the same creature who'd bounced out of our Palm Beach house one early morning years before, swinging a Grecian bell. I almost didn't know her. Felicity was heavier, squarer, with thick, dark brown hair streaked with threads of gray, and her conservative beige linen dress had a neckline that met the hollow of her throat. Only the eyes were the same: Felicity-round, as deep and brown as ever, now seeming darker, filled as they were with sadness as very slowly her lids lifted until her eyes were looking into mine. It was as though her eyes could see through mine into an area inside that was mysterious even to me.

Her hands on my cheeks were so tender they tickled. "Don't talk unless you want to," she said to me as we left Aunt Catherine and Joe. We walked out to the plane, holding hands, mute.

After we were seated and had waved once to Aunt Catherine and Joe, the motors roared and faded to a monotonous hum, and I could keep still no longer. "I do want to talk, Felicity, but I don't know how to explain this to you. I don't want to talk *about* him. I want to talk *to* him."

Her eyes were pained. "I know, Lucresse. I know that feeling."

"And I found out I *can*. You don't think that makes any sense, do you?"

"Nothing makes any sense," she said sweetly.

I grasped her hand again. "You know, I haven't cried once. Death isn't any change at all. He didn't go any place. It's just as if he was still alive, only I can't see him."

"Then there is a change, Lucresse."

"You don't understand. You don't understand the *truth!*" I snapped. "You're just like Aunt Catherine." And for the rest of the trip I treated Felicity as though she was a not particularly attractive stranger I'd been forced to sit next to. My civilities were too civil and I wouldn't offer another word having to do with the reason we were traveling together.

In the long hours of our silences, I closed my eyes, pretending to doze, and spoke to my father in my head. I told him I understood that he wouldn't be with Ben to meet us and how Felicity had changed.

"She's still better to take care of things for a while than Catherine, don't you agree?" he said. "Aren't you glad I arranged things this way?"

I had to agree, and smiled in my feigned sleep.

The body had been cremated as I'd expected. The house was still neat. Hubert padded about in his customary way. The faucets weren't a decibel less shrill; the doors still complained. Even Ben was, as I'd expected him to be—authoritative in his report, contemplative for moments at a time, but then, as interested in his own world as ever. He got Felicity to try his barbells and was gratified at how "all right" I was.

"Of course I am," I said evenly.

Suddenly, he looked alarmed. "You're *too* all right."

"I know things you don't."

Felicity gave a long sigh.

"About what? About Dad?" he pressed.

"It's the same as if he was still here—because I don't believe all the stuff Aunt Catherine does, and you both probably do. He's not flying around somewhere with wings, or jumping over live coals somewhere else."

"So what?" Ben said angrily.

"So, if he's nowhere else, he might as well be here. Don't *you* understand either? He *is*, to *me*."

I felt I was saying too much, yet I didn't care. It was time *somebody* understood—somebody besides Mrs. Dunhamly whom I might never see again.

"Lucresse, he's gone, don't you realize that?" Ben said.

"All right, where did he go?" I said defiantly.

"I don't know," Ben boomed. "But you've got to realize, he's gone. Dead. Forever."

"Those are just words. They don't mean anything, if you don't believe in heaven or hell. And Daddy didn't."

"I don't either, but there's such a thing as facing the facts."

"Yes," Felicity said heartily.

They were trying to corner me. I met the challenge head on. Triumphantly, I told them, "I've talked to him since yesterday, and he's answered me."

Ben and Felicity stared at each other. For a moment I was the outsider in the room. Then, in a flash, I knew that I, and Mrs. Dunhamly, were perhaps the only insiders on Earth where death was concerned. The billions of Christian and Jewish faithful, and all the Moslems, Hindus, Mohammedans, and Indian-lorers, and for all I knew, the Bens and Felicitys and Aunt Catherines, were the outsiders.

"I'm going to my room and talk to him now," I said. And I left them with spring in my step and new freedom in my heart, now that there was no need to hide what I knew.

Felicity had planned to stay with us for only a few days. Two days later, she changed her mind. I couldn't understand it. Though she'd been long finished with a motion picture career, she'd become entrenched as a resident of Beverly Hills and had achieved an estimable reputation as a hostess par excellence and an active participant in community affairs. "Don't you want to go back?" I asked.

"I've more important things to do here," she answered.

"We're all right. Mr. Askew at the bank is in charge of everything."

"He's not in charge of how you feel," she replied.

"I feel fine, Felicity. You can see that. And Ben's okay."

"Yes, Ben is."

Three boys from Ben's class and Louise Loder came over that evening to "pay their respects," as Louise's mother must have told her to say. They paid them with such gravity that I couldn't tolerate their attitude.

"Felicity once taught us how to do a time step. Let's turn on some music and she can teach you," I said.

"You sure you *want* to?" Louise said, surprised.

"Sure. My father would love it." I urged everybody up as I switched on the radio.

Felicity cooperated, but after the company left, she pointed her finger at me. "I wish you were plain *shicker* or plain *mashugana*, the way you're acting. But I know you're not either. All I can say is, I'm glad I'm here."

I don't know how many days passed. The duration of times of unusual emotion is always indistinct. However, I know that, for a while, I knew a mood of peace unduplicated in my life. Felicity and Ben and Hubert existed in the cloudy fringes of my attention. Much more defined was my father's voice. It began to sound without my summoning it. At odd times it summoned *my* replies.

Felicity was searching high and low for the keys to his jewelry satchel, preparatory to turning it over to a dealer designated by Mr. Askew. As I watched her rummage through his desk for the third time, he told me, "They're in the breast pocket of my brown suit."

"Oh, thanks," I said aloud. "I'll tell her."

"What?" Felicity said.

"Daddy told me they're in the breast pocket of his brown suit."

She gave me a startled look and stomped upstairs to his closet. She took the keys out of the breast pocket and whirled at me. "Sit down!"

I sat on his bed.

"You *remembered* that he kept them in that pocket, whether he was wearing that suit or not."

"No!"

"Ben!"

Ben ran in from his room, the script he'd been memorizing still in his hand.

"Tell *him*," Felicity commanded, her big brown eyes sparkling frantic.

"Felicity doesn't believe I didn't *remember* where Daddy's satchel keys were. I *didn't* remember. He *told* me."

"Do you think I ought to phone my old head man?" Felicity asked Ben.

"Lucresse," Ben said, "I hate to do this to you, but it's got to be done. Come here."

He led *me* and Felicity downstairs to the spot in the living room where the marble-topped table had been.

"I'll be Dad," he said. "We were bending over the table this way. I was approximately where Felicity is..." Felicity moved to the sofa and leaned against its arm. "Hubert was on the long end, over there. We lifted once, about two inches. His face got red, and he gasped..."

Ben's head jerked back, as though thrown by the force of the rushing air he gulped in. His resemblance to my father was uncanny. Even his trousers looked baggy.

"I let down my end and said, 'Are you all right?' He started to lift again..."

"Ben, stop!" Felicity cried.

I drew my breath with difficulty.

Ben didn't stop. "He dropped his end, just let go... it's a wonder the whole top didn't crack in two. His hands just fell, didn't even try to break his fall. He collapsed right about here..."

Ben, reverting to Ben, indicated a body's length area on the floor.

"We carried him to the sofa. His suit jacket dragged on the floor... I stepped on one of the buttons as we carried him. Hubert ran to the phone and called a doctor. I kept squeezing his face. He looked sick to his stomach, but he didn't vomit. Without opening his eyes, he said, 'Get Felicity to bring Lucresse back. Be nice to her, Ben..."

A shudder swept through me. Ben's voice was too the same as the voice I'd known all my life, the voice that had never stopped speaking to me.

"Then it was over. In an hour, the doctor had been there, I had called Mr. Askew, who called the men from the crematorium. They took him out...I didn't go.

"Before I called either of you, two fellows came with the transport truck and crated the table top. They lifted it with no trouble at all. And that was all. It was gone. And *he* was gone. Now, do you understand?"

My hands dug into my temples, trying to make my brain understand. "If I could have *seen* him..." I said.

"Be glad you didn't."

Felicity touched my arm and said to Ben, "No, you're wrong."

She took me to my room. "Rest a while," she said. "We're going out later."

I didn't ask where. I didn't care. Whatever she wanted to do was all right with me, as long as she'd leave me alone now so I could talk to my father and get back my bearings. I closed my door after her, with a slam.

"Ben's a pretty good actor," I said. "You always said so."

My father's voice was weaker than before. "I always said he'd be a success."

"Sometimes I can't tell whether he's acting or not."

"Good acting always has some truth to it."

"Was he telling the truth just now?"

"People can only tell the truth as they see it. And everyone sees it differently."

"Then *I'd* have seen it differently. I *do* see it differently," I said victoriously.

Felicity knocked at my door and came in before I could admit her. "Do you have a hat?" she asked excitedly.

"No."

"We're going somewhere where you need one." She disappeared and returned with a fourth-moon black straw piece with a short veil. "Wear this, and something dark."

Again I didn't ask where we were going.

Ben drove us to a church at the bottom of the hill, near the station. No one said anything on the way except Felicity's, "Lucky there *was* one today. I hope we aren't late."

All the people entering the church were smiling sadly to each other. A somber attendant ushered us to a back pew without asking who we were. Centered on the altar was an open coffin. A bald minister appeared at the lectern behind it. He monotoned some responsive readings, and more energetically, sailed into a lengthy eulogy. We sat in silence. Though I listened carefully, I didn't feel that I knew any more about the body in the coffin at the end of his speech than I'd known at the beginning, except that it was a man's. I wanted to leave.

Ben held me back. "We're going to see it," he whispered.

My arms became bumped with tiny, tingling pimples in the warmth of the consecrating hall. I thought of Mrs. Dunhamly. This was the kind of spectacle she found rewarding enough to be almost enjoyable.

Ben nudged me and I got into line behind Felicity to stroll with the crowd up to the bier. I raised the veil on my hat.

There was an astonishing display inside the coffin. The face facing mine wasn't old, wasn't young, it wasn't any age. It wasn't happy, wasn't sad, wasn't peaceful or sleepy; it wasn't even definitely male or female. It was ageless, genderless, a grotesque creation of some artless beautician. Suddenly, it assumed my father's features—only his features, none of his life. No matter who it had been, a stranger or my father, it was what Mrs. Dunhamly meant by the Nothing of Death.

"You haven't gone anywhere *else*," I pled into the gaping box.

"Move on," Felicity said, pulling at my sleeve.

I moved on, and had to wait behind Felicity for a woman way ahead and another much older woman to move before everyone else. They were the family. I wondered if they recognized the occupant of the coffin as having been someone they'd known.

We went home, in silence again. In my room, I implored, "Daddy, you couldn't be like that..."

There was no answer.

Maybe Aunt Catherine had been right: maybe Mrs. Dunhamly *was* a poor soul—unable to accept the misery in living—and I wasn't sure how harmless she was. But maybe she wasn't harmful. This was too confusing. I tried once more.

"Daddy, *did* Ben tell the truth?"

Again, there was no answer. And no answer. And no answer.

An hour was a long time ago, way back when I was innocent—as innocent and self-deceiving as bad actors like Aunt Catherine or good ones like Ben. Actors who told only some of the truth: black-or-white and here-or-there half-truths, truths like the "everywhere" I used to handle the truths of "not here" and "nothingness" without sobbing.

I walked through the house, ignoring Felicity and Ben, knowing I would never talk to my father again, and that I'd never be free from the knowledge that he was no longer here.

I walked upstairs. Then I walked downstairs. I walked and walked and walked till I roared. Then I roared till I sobbed.

Then I wept into Felicity's lap through half that night.

AFTERTHOUGHTS

It may seem that Ben and I were bequeathed a harder heritage than many, without the cushions of faith and family to dull the sharp surfaces of the adult world we were moving into. Nevertheless, we moved into it faster than most. We had the Winding Hill noisy house to come home to until I finished college, and Ben completed two years each of college and drama school. Then, with no regrets, we entered other, separate worlds.

Ben's was fame and fortune, acting in the theater and movie and TV studios. But he married a girl who admired him more when he wasn't acting than when he was. He truly wanted what he had. I chose a fellow who had all my own insecurities and wonder, even though his family had lived in one house all his life. I suppose I, too, got what I wanted. We've already moved three times, once for each of our children. Ben and his wife and two boys live in a number of places, wherever he's working. We all call it traveling, not moving. Perhaps that reflects the trouble with the truth we still have on some subjects.

Felicity visits or calls on special occasions and when she gets the yen. Fred, who's ninety-three, miraculously made it through the war years fairly unscathed and still walks once each day, very slowly now, to the statue in the center of his village square. He writes to me or Ben every few months—in a sweet, scolding tone that makes us feel like children again. Every December 22nd, we each receive a

Christmas card from Aunt Catherine with a squeezed, worried note on the plain side above the imprinted price mark. And I think of her visits over the years.

I don't often see anybody who reminds me of Sled-boy or Miss Bunce or Arthur Frith, or Mrs. Loder or Lois Carrington. Unless I happen to be thinking of them.

But *everywhere* I see people who remind me of my father. "People can only tell the truth as they see it" were his last words to me. And I see my father everywhere. So, thinking of what I just wrote, maybe I have no trouble with the truth after all.

ABOUT THE AUTHORS

Edna Robinson (1921–1990) lived all over the U.S. and attended twenty-seven schools before the eighth grade. Early on, she wrote for radio soaps and small-town newspapers' "Society News." After graduating from Northwestern University in 1943, she headed for New York City, and in the pre-*Mad Men* days of advertising, she became not only one of the first female copywriters, but one of the only Jewish copywriters. When directed to the typing pool, she simply refused to accept that being a secretary was her only option and she declared her intention to write. Fortunately her first boss found such hubris charming and he became her mentor. While working at ad agencies, she developed a number of well-known advertising lines ("Navigators of the world since it was flat"; "A kid'll eat the middle of an Oreo first..."; and "Nutter Butter Peanut Butter Cookies") and developed new products. She also wrote feature articles for horse magazines and *Sports Illustrated*, children's books for Hallmark, and short stories for adults. She had a lifelong love of music that began at the age of twelve, when she wandered into a piano teacher's house, saw a piano, and declared that she just knew she could play it. This turned out to be true, and after studying piano for fifteen months, Edna began concertizing and was lauded as a child prodigy. About a year later, she stopped playing when she moved away from her beloved teacher. She was the mother of four children.

Betsy Robinson is a freelance editor, novelist, journalist, playwright, and former actor. Her novel *The Last Will & Testament of Zelda McFigg*, winner of Black Lawrence Press's Big Moose Prize, was published in September 2014. In 2001, her novel *Plan Z by Leslie Kove* was published by Mid-List Press, as winner of their First Novel Series award. In her late twenties, Betsy and her mother, Edna, became best friends and eventually writing partners. In 2011, Betsy published a book of letters between herself and her dead mother, *Conversations with Mom: An Aging Baby Boomer, in Need of an Elder, Writes to Her Dead Mother.* She had teamed with Edna to write screenplays under a 1987/88 Writers Guild East Foundation Fellowship and was elated to relive the partnership through imagined letters and, even more viscerally, through her work on *The Trouble with the Truth*. Learn more at www.BetsyRobinson-writer.com.

ACKNOWLEDGMENTS

Since Edna Robinson died in 1990, I—her daughter, editor, and friend, Betsy—would like to acknowledge Edna for this beautiful book. I acknowledge her talent, her furious determination, and her courage to go on, no matter what it took—to survive, to live joyfully, and, most of all, to change.

I would like to thank Stephen Camilli for being excited by my first lunatic pitch of this book when he happened by the Editorial Freelancers Association booth at BookExpo America. Thank you for being such an open, honest, and loving person. And thank you, Sara Camilli, for being my agent and finding this book a home.

There is no way to fully express my gratitude to Infinite Words for doing what publishers never do—accepting a book by a dead author.

And thank you to all the readers. Even though Edna is no longer in body, I believe she is dancing and laughing and maybe giving you a hug.